BAD BU$INESS

Robert B. Parker

BAD BUSINESS

G. P. PUTNAM'S SONS

New York

G. P. Putnam's Sons
Publishers Since 1838
a member of
Penguin Group (USA) Inc.
375 Hudson Street
New York, NY 10014

Library of Congress Cataloging-in-Publication Data
Parker, Robert B., date.
Bad business / Robert B. Parker.
p.   cm.
ISBN 0-399-15145-1
1. Spenser (Fictitious character)—Fiction.   2. Private
investigators—Massachusetts—Boston—Fiction.   3. Boston
(Mass.)—Fiction.   I. Title.
PS3566.A686B34   2004   2003063251
813'.54—dc22

Printed in the United States of America
3   5   7   9   10   8   6   4

This book is printed on acid-free paper. ♾

BOOK DESIGN BY AMANDA DEWEY

FOR JOAN:

good business

BAD BU$INESS

1

D o you do divorce work?" the woman said.

"I do," I said.

"Are you any good?"

"I am," I said.

"I don't want likelihood," she said. "Or guesswork. I need evidence that will stand up in court."

"That's not up to me," I said. "That's up to the evidence."

She sat quietly in my client chair and thought about that.

"You're telling me you won't manufacture it," she said.

"Yes," I said.

"You won't have to," she said. "The sonovabitch can't keep his dick in his pants for a full day."

"Must make dining out a little awkward," I said.

She ignored me. I was used to it. Mostly I amused myself.

"I always have trouble convincing people that any man would cheat on a woman like me. I mean, look at me."

"Unbelievable," I said.

"My attorneys tell me you are too expensive," she said. "But that you are probably worth it."

"The same could be remarked of Susan Silverman."

She frowned.

"Who the hell is Susan Silverman?" she said.

"Girl of my dreams."

She frowned again. Then she said, "Oh, I see. You're being cute."

"It's my nature," I said.

"Well, it's not mine," she said. "Do you want the job?"

"Sure."

"My attorneys will want a strict accounting of what you spend," she said.

"I'll bet they will," I said.

She was good-looking in kind of an old-fashioned way. Sort of womanly. Before personal trainers, and StairMasters. Like the women in *Life* Magazine when we were all much younger. Like she would look good in a small-waisted white polka-dot dress, and a huge straw hat with a white polka-dot band. In fact, of course, she was wearing a beige pantsuit and big pearls. Her reddish blond hair was long and thoroughly sprayed, and framed her face like the halo in a mediaeval religious painting. Her mouth was kind of thin and her eyes were small. I imagined cheating on her.

"I'm represented by Frampton and Keyes," she said. "Do you know the firm?"

"I don't."

"You'll do all further business through them. The managing partner is Randy Frampton."

"Why didn't you let them hire me," I said.

"I don't let other people make judgments for me. I wanted to look you in the eye."

I nodded.

"Do you have pictures of your husband?" I said. "Names of suspected paramours? Addresses? That sort of thing?"

"You can get all that from Randy."

"And a retainer?"

"Randy will take care of that as well."

"Good for Randy," I said. "Will he tell me your name, too?"

"I'd rather keep that confidential for now," she said. "This is a very sensitive situation."

I smiled.

"Ma'am," I said. "How long do you think it will take me to find out your name once I know who your husband is?"

"I . . ."

I smiled my sunny good-natured smile at her. I could melt polar ice caps with my sunny good-natured smile. She was no match for it.

"Marlene," she said. "Marlene Rowley. My husband is Trenton Rowley."

"How do you do," I said. "My name is Spenser."

"Of course I know your name," she said. "How do you think I got here?"

"I thought you looked up handsome in the phone book," I said. "And my picture was there."

She smiled for the first time that morning.

"Well," she said. "Maybe you are a little bit handsome in a rough sort of way."

"Tough," I said. "But sensitive."

"Perhaps," she said. "Will you speak with Randy?"

"Right away," I said.

2

Frampton and Keyes had offices on the second floor of a two-story building in downtown Beverly. It was one of those block-long brick buildings built before the Second World War when most of the bigger towns were discrete entities rather than suburbs of Boston. There was less open space than you found in the big Boston firms. More small offices, but no partitioned cubbies. In the small reception area was a four-foot-long model of a clipper ship. There were paintings of ships on the walls. The magazines on the small reading table were devoted to golf and sailing.

At the reception desk was a young woman with a big chest and a small sweater, who probably wasn't devoted to golf and sailing. She smiled at me happily as I came in. I suspected that she smiled at most men happily.

"My name is Spenser," I said. "To see Randy Frampton."

"Concerning?" she said.

"I'm trying to establish if that's his first name or a descriptive adjective," I said.

She looked at me and frowned for a minute and then smiled widely.

"That is most definitely his first name, Mr. Spenser. Is there anything else you need to see Mr. Frampton about?"

"Tell him Marlene Rowley sent me," I said.

"Yes sir," she said and smiled at me and her eyes were lively.

Randy Frampton, the managing partner, had a corner office. Randy was not very tall. His weight was disproportionate to his height. He had gray hair that needed cutting. His dark blue suit needed pressing and wasn't much better than the one I owned. His tie was yellow silk, and he wore a white broadcloth shirt with one collar point slightly askew. I couldn't see because he was behind his desk, but I suspected that his shoes weren't shined.

"So she decided to hire you," Frampton said.

"Who wouldn't?" I said.

Frampton sighed a little.

"Marlene is sometimes erratic," he said. "Did she instruct you that everything goes through this firm?"

"Yeah," I said. "But I'm not sure she meant it."

Frampton smiled pleasantly.

"That sounds like Marlene," he said. "But I mean it. You and I need to be on the same page."

"She was pretty clear that you took care of paying me," I said.

"You'll submit your expenses, carefully kept, weekly, and we'll pay them weekly. When the investigation is complete, you'll submit your final bill. Shall we discuss rates?"

I told him my rates. He shook his head.

"I'm sorry, but that's out of line."

"Sure," I said.

"We'll need to negotiate that a little."

"Nope," I said.

"You won't negotiate?"

"Nope."

"Then I'm afraid we can't do business," Frampton said.

"Okay," I said, and stood up. "You want to tell Marlene, or shall I."

"That's it?" Frampton said. "No discussion? Nothing?"

"Marlene doesn't look like she'll be fun to work for," I said.

"You require fun?"

"Fun or money," I said.

Frampton sat back in his chair and swiveled away from me and looked out his window.

"You know you've got me over a barrel," he said.

"I do."

"You know I don't want to tell Marlene that we wouldn't hire you."

"I know," I said.

"Will you require a contract?"

"Handshake's fine," I said.

"That's foolish," he said. "You should have a contract."

"I know," I said. "I just wanted to see your reaction."

Frampton looked at me thoughtfully.

"You are a little different," he said. "Aren't you?"

All the answers to that question seemed dumb, so I didn't give one.

"We'll draft a contract and you can run it past your attorney," Frampton said.

"Okay."

"Are you prepared to begin now?" Frampton said.

"Sure."

"Very well," he said. "What do you know."

"Marlene wants me to catch her husband cheating on her."

"Anything else?"

"Nope."

"What would you like from me?"

"Her husband's name; his address, home and business; a couple of different pictures of him; description of his car, plate number. And maybe your reaction to her suspicions."

He reached into a file drawer and took out a big manila envelope and tossed it on his desk in front of me.

"Pictures," he said. "Of Trenton Rowley. He's forty-seven years old. He and Marlene live here, in Manchester. The address is in the envelope. So is his business address. He has several cars, I don't know what kind. I don't have the plate numbers. His business is off Totten Pond Road in Waltham. Company named Kinergy, got their own building."

"Kinergy?" I said.

Frampton shrugged.

"I have no idea what it means," he said.

"What do they do?"

"Energy trading of some kind," Frampton said.

"That doesn't mean they run a power plant," I said.

"No, no. They're traders—brokers. They buy power here and sell it there."

"Gee," I said. "Just like the legislature."

Frampton smiled a little.

"Kinergy," he said, "is an enormously successful company."

"And what does he do there?"

"He's the chief financial officer."

"Mr. Rowley is wealthy?"

"Yes. And he has a lot of clout."

"Yikes," I said. "Do you folks represent him as well?"

"Oh God no. Obviously we couldn't represent both sides in a divorce, but, even if we could. No, no. The company does business with Cone, Oakes, and Baldwin. I would assume they might represent him as well."

"What about the last part of my question?"

"What do I think?"

I nodded.

"Trent Rowley has, for a long time, gotten everything he wanted. He has always given Marlene everything she wanted."

"So do you think he's cheating on her?"

"I don't know. I think he would if he wanted to."

"Marlene have any evidence?"

"I don't know. She says she knows he's cheating. But she adds nothing of substance to the accusation."

"Doe she have much of substance?"

"In this case?"

"In any case," I said.

Frampton shook his head slowly.

"Marlene is a client," he said. "It is unbecoming an attorney to discuss his clients' personal quirks."

"Heavens," I said. "Integrity?"

"One finds it in the most unlikely places," Frampton said. "Even, now and then, in law firms."

"I'm heartened," I said.

3

I took Rita Fiore to dinner at the Federalist. Rita was the chief criminal litigator at Cone, Oakes. But I had known her since she was an ADA in Norfolk County, and, in a healthy platonic fashion, we liked each other.

"How's your love life," I said after we'd each gotten a martini.

"Busy," she said." But, same old question—why are there so many more horses' asses than there are horses?"

"Still looking for Mr. Right?"

"Always. I thought I had him last year. Chief of police on the North Shore."

"But?"

"But he had an ex-wife."

"And?"

"And he wouldn't let go."

"Oh well," I said.

"Yeah. That may become the Fiore family motto."

"And the previous Mr. Right?" I said. "Number, what was it, five?"

"Divorce is final." She grinned at me. "I cleaned his clock too."

"I'd have expected no less," I said. "What do you know about Trent Rowley?"

"He's the CFO at Kinergy. Whom we represent."

"Tell me about him?"

"Discussing a client is considered unethical."

I nodded. The waiter brought menus. We read them and ordered.

"May I bring you another cocktail?" he said.

Rita smiled up at him.

"Oh, please," she said.

"You, sir?"

"He'll have one too," Rita said.

"Very good."

The waiter picked up the menus and smiled at Rita and left.

"Our waiter is hot for you," I said.

"Wow," Rita said. "A straight waiter."

"Maybe he's Mr. Right," I said.

"Can't be. For one thing a waiter can't swathe me in luxury. And secondly, if they're hot for me that proves they're Mr. Wrong."

"Maybe you should stop getting married and just sleep with people."

"I'm doing that too," Rita said. "Except you."

"My loss," I said. "What about Trent Rowley?"

"What about client confidentiality?"

"What about several martinis and dinner?" I said.

The waiter came with our second martinis. Rita sipped hers happily.

"You think you can bribe me," she said, "with a few martinis and some Chilean sea bass?"

"I do," I said.

Our salads arrived. Rita picked up a scrap of Boston lettuce in her fingers and nibbled on it. Susan was the only other person I knew who could eat with her fingers and look elegant.

"Why do you want to know about him?" Rita said. "Why not just catch him in the act? Tell the little woman, collect your fee, and stand by to testify at the divorce proceedings."

"Excuse to have dinner with you, Toots."

"Like you need an excuse."

"I like to have an idea of what I'm dealing with. It was time for us to have dinner again. It seemed a nice synergy."

"You are a bear for knowing things," Rita said.

"Knowledge is power," I said.

Rita drank some more of her martini. Her big greenish eyes softened a little. They always did when she drank. She had thick red hair and great legs, and was smarter than Bill Gates.

"We have a whole department servicing Kinergy," Rita said. "I talked to the lead guy, Tom Clark. He says that there isn't anything to know about Rowley outside of business hours. Rowley starts early, works late, and, as far as Tom knows, has no other life."

"Doesn't sound like Mr. Right to me," I said.

"Apparently Mrs. Rowley doesn't think so either."

I shrugged.

"Maybe she wants out," I said. "But she wants to take half of everything with her."

"Can't blame a girl for trying," Rita said. "In my last divorce, I didn't, of course, settle for half."

"Marlene may be less experienced," I said.

"Marlene?"

"Someone named Rita is making fun of a name like Marlene?"

"I don't get the chance that often," Rita said.

The salad plates disappeared. The entrees came. The waiter took a bottle of sauvignon blanc from the ice bucket and poured a little for Rita to sample. She said it was drinkable and he poured some out for each of us.

"So he's a big success," I said.

"Oh, you bet. Kinergy is a huge profit machine."

"Just from brokering energy?"

"Sure," Rita said. "You are running short of electrical power in your grid, they can acquire some from another source, reroute it to you, and charge you a fortune. Like the power shortfall in California, couple years ago."

"Is it that simple?"

"At bottom a lot of businesses are simple. You know. American Airlines picks you up in Boston and flies you to LA. That's the service. The complicated part comes in how to do it profitably."

"Can they manipulate the market?"

"Probably."

"Do they?"

"Probably. Tom sees very little evil in a client," Rita said, "and speaks less."

"Does he gossip?"

"Not to me," Rita said. "Not about clients. He swears there is nothing to gossip about with Rowley."

"You believe him?"

"Tom's a company guy. And he wants to be managing partner. The firm says jump and he says 'how high?' "

"Which means if Rowley says jump . . ."

" 'How high,' " Rita said. "Can we talk about sex again?"

"We'd be fools not to," I said.

4

At 6 A.M., drinking a large coffee to help my heart get started, I drove out the Mass Pike and south on 128 to Waltham. The Kinergy Building was just off Route 128. It was innovatively ugly: five different kinds of brick facings, intermingled with black glass and textured concrete, sporting a multilevel profile. It looked like Darth Vader's country home.

Near the front entrance were parking spots labeled CEO, COO, CFO. I parked in the visitors slot and waited to see if I could get a live look at Trent Rowley when he came to work. I was there in place, on the alert, at 6:10. I was just in time. At 6:15 a silver BMW sports car pulled into the CFO parking space and Rowley got out.

He looked just like his picture: strong jaw, dark wavy hair

worn longish. He had on small round glasses with thin gold frames. He was crisp and clean and pressed and tailored in a tan summer suit, a blue shirt with a pin collar, and a pale blue tie. He almost certainly smelled of expensive cologne. He walked very briskly into the still empty building, proud of being the earliest bird.

What kind of affair can a guy have when he shows up for work at 6:15 in the morning?

I hung around until everyone else came to work, without seeing anyone who looked like they might be having an affair with Rowley. Though it was, admittedly, hard to be sure. Then I wrote down the plate number on the BMW. That done, I still had some energy left over, so I drove back to Boston and went to the gym.

At four in the afternoon, sound of muscle and pure of mind, with a tall can of Budweiser to replenish my electrolytes, I drove back to Kinergy and waited for Rowley to come out. By the time he did it was nearly eight o'clock. I was thinking deeply about a sub sandwich and another beer. I followed him north on Route 128, to Route 2, and in Route 2 to Cambridge. We went along the river to the Hyatt Hotel, where Rowley turned off and drove into the parking garage, behind the hotel.

I left my car and twenty bucks with the doorman, and was in the lobby hanging around near the elevators when Rowley came in. He was carrying a small overnight bag, and paying me no attention as he headed to the elevator. The Hyatt has one of those twenty-story Portman lobbies, where you reach your floor by a glass-enclosed elevator, and each room door opens out onto an interior balcony overlooking the lobby. He went to the seventh floor and got out and walked to his left, halfway down the balcony, and knocked on a door. The door opened and in he went. I looked at my watch. It was ten minutes of nine, and Rowley's evening was just starting. It made me feel old.

I took the elevator to the seventh floor, and walked down to the twelfth door to the left, which was where Rowley had knocked. It was room number 717. I wrote it down and went back downstairs and took a seat in the lobby near the elevators, across from a little guy with a big nose. He was wearing a tan windbreaker and reading the paper. He was seriously engaged with his newspaper. Now and then as he read he'd smile or frown or shake his head. I on the other hand was seriously engaged in looking at the people who came and went into and out of the elevator. In my first hour I saw three women who passed muster, one of whom was a rare sighting. She earned nine on a scale where Susan was ten. I could hear the piano in the cocktail lounge. By 11:15 the foot traffic had thinned at the elevator. I had turned to thinking about my all-fathers-and-sons baseball team. The little guy with the big nose had finally given up on the newspaper and appeared to be whistling silently. *Songs unheard are sweeter far.* I had gotten as far as Dick Sisler at first when the door to room 717 opened and Trent Rowley came out with a woman. The woman was carrying a large purse with a shoulder strap. They walked to the elevator and came down. She looked good getting off the elevator. Short blond hair brushed back. Good body, maybe a little heavy in the legs, but nothing to disqualify her. Her eyes were made up and her lipstick looked fresh. Despite that, I thought there was some sort of postcoital blur in her expression. It might not stand up in court, but it was an expression I'd seen elsewhere.

I wasn't wrong. They walked past us toward the corridor that led to the parking garage. I got up as soon as they passed and hot-footed it down to get my car from the doorman. The little guy with the nose was right behind me. We looked at each other while the doorman got our car keys.

"You're following her," I said.

He grinned.

"And you're following him."

I grinned.

"And now we'll switch," I said.

He nodded.

"You'll follow her home, and I'll follow him home. And then we'll know who's who."

"Might be easier," I said, "to pool information."

"Nope," the little guy said, "got to be done right."

The little guy took a business card out of his shirt pocket.

"But maybe we can talk later." He handed me the card. "Save you from chasing down my registration."

I took his card and gave him one of mine and we both got in our cars as Rowley pulled out of the parking garage. The little guy gave me a thumbs-up gesture and pulled out behind Rowley and drove off after him. I did the same with the woman.

5

The little guy's name was Elmer O'Neill, and his card said
he conducted discreet inquiries. Me too. He arrived at my
office the next morning right after I did.

"You got any coffee?" he said.

"I'm about to make some," I said.

"Good."

He sat in one of my client chairs with his legs crossed, while
I measured the coffee into the filter basket and the water into
the reservoir and turned on the coffeemaker.

"Your name's Spenser," he said.

"Yep."

"You know mine."

"I do."

The coffeemaker gurgled encouragingly. I put out two coffee mugs and two spoons, and some sugar, and a small carton of half-and-half. Elmer looked around my office.

"You must be doing okay," he said.

"Because my office is so elegant?" I said.

"Naw. The place is a dump. But the location—must cost you some rent."

"Dump seems harsh," I said.

Elmer made a gesture with his hand as if he were shooing a fly.

"It's why I'm in Arlington," he said. "Costs a lot less and I can still get in town quick when I need to."

The coffee was done. I poured it out.

"You find out my client's name yet?" I said.

"He lives in Manchester," Elmer said. "And after we talk I can check his plates at the registry."

I nodded.

"His name is Trenton Rowley," I said. "He's the CFO of a company in Waltham called Kinergy."

Elmer nodded as if that meant something to him. He set his coffee cup on the edge of my desk, took out a small notebook, and wrote it down.

"Who's the woman?" I said.

"Ellen Eisen," he said. "Husband works the same place."

"Kinergy?"

"Un-huh."

"And they live in the new Ritz condos off Tremont Street."

"And you were going to check her plates at the registry if I didn't tell you."

"Might anyway," I said.

"Shit," Elmer said. "You don't trust me?"

"He hire you?" I said.

"Yep. Rowley's wife hire you?"

"Un-huh."

Elmer leaned back a little in his chair so that the front legs cleared the floor. He rocked the chair slightly with his toes.

"Well," he said. "We know they're fucking."

"We know they spent time together in a hotel room," I said.

"Oh hell," Elmer said. "A purist."

"Didn't you say everything had to be done right?"

"That's because I didn't know if I could trust you."

"How unkind," I said. "My client will want something more solid than the shared hotel room. She plans to 'get-everything-he-has-the-philandering-bastard.' "

"My guy just wants to know is she cheating on him," Elmer said.

"His name is Eisen?"

"Yeah, sure."

"Sometimes women keep their, ah, premarital name," I said.

"Ain't that horseshit," Elmer said. "Guy's name is Bernard Eisen. He's COO at, whatsitsname, Kinergy."

"Small world," I said.

"So," he said. "I guess we should tell the clients."

"I'd like to let themselves dig a deeper hole," I said.

He drank a little more coffee.

"That's 'cause your client wants more than mine does."

"True," I said. "But if you tell yours then I probably won't be able to get what my client wants."

"But my client will settle for what I know now."

"An ethical dilemma," I said.

Elmer frowned a little.

"Don't run into many of them anymore," he said. "You got more coffee?"

I poured him another cup. He added a lot of sugar and half-and-half, stirred it slowly.

"There's another little thing," he said.

"Well," I said. "Two cups of coffee ought to buy me something."

He grinned.

"Somebody seems to be tailing Mrs. Rowley, too."

6

Susan and I were sitting on a stone pier at the beach in Kennebunkport, looking at the ocean and eating lunch out of a wicker basket.

"So," she said, "if I understand it. You are, on behalf of Mrs. Rowley, trailing Mr. Rowley, who is having a clandestine affair with Mrs. Eisen, who is being followed by Elmer O'Neill on behalf of Mr. Eisen."

"Exactly," I said.

Susan had a lobster club sandwich, which she ate by taking the two slices of bread apart and eating the various components of the sandwich separately, slowly, and in very small bites.

"And after their rendezvous, for purposes of identification, you trailed Mrs. Eisen home . . ."

"To the new Ritz."

She ate a piece of bacon from the sandwich. I had a pastrami on light rye, which I ate in the conventional manner.

"And Mr. O'Neill trailed Mr. Rowley home."

"Yes."

"And encountered someone conducting surveillance on Mrs. Rowley."

"Yes."

"How hideous," Susan said.

"Hideous?"

"A gaggle of private detectives," she said. "You assume that Mr. Rowley is also trying to catch Mrs. Rowley?"

"I do," I said.

Susan ate a part of a lettuce leaf. A fishing boat chugged in toward the river past us, a boy at the wheel. A man stood next to him. We watched as they passed.

"A veritable circle jerk," Susan said.

"Wow," I said, "you shrinks have a technical language all your own, don't you?"

"Bet your ass," Susan said. "Do you know the identity of the third snoop?"

"No. Elmer didn't get the plate numbers."

I ate my half-sour pickle and looked at the dark water moving against the great granite blocks below us.

Susan said, "None of this changes what you were hired to do, of course."

"Of course."

"Do what you were hired to do, collect your pay, and move on."

"Yep."

The movement of the immediate water sort of dragged me

outward toward a bigger and bigger seascape until I felt the near eternal presence of the ocean far past the horizon.

"But you won't," Susan said.

"I won't?"

"Nope."

We had a couple of bottles of Riesling. I poured us some wine.

"A jug of wine, some plastic cups, and thou," I said.

"You will have to know if Mr. Rowley hired someone to follow Mrs. Rowley and if so, why."

"I will?"

"Yes."

"Why is that?" I said.

"Because of how you are. When you pick something up, you can't put it down until you know it entirely," Susan said. "Your imagination simply won't let go of it, and, whether you want to or not, you'll be turning it every which way to see what it's made of."

"Do you have a diagnosis?"

"It's what in my profession we call characterological."

"Which means you haven't an explanation."

"Basically yes," Susan said. "It's simply how you are."

"You sure?"

"Yes."

"Because you know me so well?"

She smiled. "Yes."

"And . . . ?" I said.

She smiled wider.

"Because that's how I am too."

"Makes you good at what you do," I said.

"Makes both of us good," Susan said. "We are hounds for the truth."

"Woof," I said.

We sat with our shoulders touching and our backs to the land, and ate our lunch, and drank our wine, and felt the pull of the ocean's implacable kinesis.

"Should we walk back to the White Barn and have a nap?" I said. "And afterwards a swim in the pool, and cocktails, and dinner?"

"Is 'nap' a euphemism for something more active?" Susan said.

"The two are not mutually exclusive," I said.

"No," Susan. "But its important that they don't coincide."

Which they didn't.

7

H ere's the deal," I said to Elmer. "You stay with Ellen Eisen, and let me know if she meets my guy, and I'll see what I can find out about who's watching Mrs. Rowley."

"Whadda you care who's watching Mrs. Rowley?"

"It's characterological," I said.

"Sure it is," Elmer said. "I'll buy in if I get something out of it."

"I'll owe you," I said.

"If finding out gets you any money," Elmer said, "half of it's mine."

"You bet," I said.

"Can I trust you," Elmer said.

"You bet," I said.

He looked at me for a time without saying anything. His little dark eyes were slightly oval, as if, maybe, a long way back, one of the O'Neills had been Asian. Finally he nodded to himself slowly.

"Yeah," he said. "Your word is good."

"How do you know that?" I said.

"I know," Elmer said. "I'll keep in touch."

He got up and went toward the door. He walked with a little swagger. He would have walked with a big swagger had he been larger. Pearl the Wonder Dog II stood up on the office sofa and stared at Elmer as he walked past. She didn't bristle, but she didn't wag her tail either.

"Fucking dog don't like me," he said.

"She's just cautious," I said. "She hasn't been with us very long."

"He some kinda Doberman?"

"She's a German shorthaired pointer," I said.

"Same thing," Elmer said.

I walked over and sat on the couch beside Pearl, and she stretched up her neck to give me a lap.

"Now's your chance," I said. "Make a break for it."

After Elmer made his escape, Pearl and I sat on the couch for a while until I was sure Elmer hadn't hurt her feelings. Then I took her to Susan's house. Susan was seeing patients on the first floor. Pearl ran up the stairs to the second floor where Susan lived. When I opened the door she raced into Susan's bedroom, jumped on the bed, clamped onto one of the pillows, and subdued it ferociously. Her self-esteem seemed intact. I gave her a cookie, made sure there was water, left a note on the front hall table for Susan, and went to Manchester.

Set well back from the road, on a corner lot, devoid of foun-
dation plantings, the Rowley house was as big and costly and
ugly as anything north of Boston. Postmodern, the designer
probably said. The look of the twenty-first century without sac-
rificing the values of the past, he probably insisted. I thought
it looked like a house assembled by a committee. There were
dormers and columns and niches, and peaks and porches and
round windows and a roof line that fluctuated like my income.
In the front yard there were no flowers, shrubs, or trees. Just a
long dull inexpensive sweep of recently cut grass, traversed by
a hot top driveway that led to a turnaround apron in front of
the garage. It was as if they'd run out of money after the house

was built. The place was painted an exciting white. With imaginative gray shutters.

I parked around the corner on the side street where I could see Rowley's driveway through the shade trees along the road. I played my new Gerry Mulligan/Chet Baker CD. I sang along a little with Chet. *They're writing songs of love, but not for me . . .* Then I played Lee Wiley and Bobby Hackett. At 4:30 in the afternoon a silver Lexus SUV came down the street and pulled into the driveway. It parked at the head of the driveway and Marlene got out, carrying a pale pink garment bag. A dark maroon Chevy sedan came down the street in the same direction Marlene had come from, and turned in onto my side street. The driver looked at me carefully as he passed. I read his registration in my rearview mirror, a trick that always impressed people, and wrote it down. Maybe fifty yards up the street he U-turned and parked behind me.

We sat. I listened to some Dean Martin. I always thought he sounded like me. Susan has always said he didn't. Some starlings were working the lawn in front of the Rowleys' house, and two chickadees. I turned Dean down, and called Frank Belson on my car phone and got shuffled around the homicide division for about five minutes before I got him.

"Can you check a car registration for me," I said.

"Of course," he said. "I welcome the chance to do real police work."

"Don't let them push you around at the Registry," I said, and gave him the number and hung up. In my rearview mirror I could see the guy behind me on his car phone. I smiled. Pretty soon we'd know each other's name. I listened some more to

Dino, and watched the birds foraging on the lawn some more until Belson called me back.

"Car's registered to the Templeton Group, one hundred Summer Street," Belson said.

"Company car," I said.

"Unless there's some guy walking around named Templeton Group."

"You know what the company does?"

"I figured you'd ask so I used a special investigative tool known only to law enforcement."

"You looked them up in the phone book."

"I did. Detective agency."

"Of course it's a detective agency," I said.

"You owe me two martinis and a steak," Belson said.

"Put it on my account," I said.

"There's no room left on your account," Belson said and hung up.

I called Rita Fiore.

"Cone, Oakes use a particular detective agency?" I said.

"That's it?" Rita said. "No 'hello you sexy thing, who does Cone, Oakes use?' "

"Who do they use?" I said.

"I use you."

"I know, but who, for divorce work, say, or corporate crime?"

"I do criminal litigation, for crissake. I don't know who the white collar doo doos use."

"You could ask."

"And call you back?"

"Exactly," I said. "You sexy thing."

Rita hung up. I put in my CD of Benny Goodman's 1938

Carnegie Hall Jazz Concert. We were halfway through Avalon when Rita called back.

"Lawton Associates," she said. "Big firm on Broad Street. I'm told they're very discreet."

"Unlike yourself," I said.

Rita laughed and hung up. She had a great laugh. I thought about things for a little while. Whoever had hired the Templeton Group probably hadn't done it through Cone, Oakes. Didn't mean it wasn't somebody at Kinergy. But it didn't mean it was. I always hated clues that didn't tell you anything. I thought about things some more. After a while, I got sick of that, and decided to do something instead of doing nothing, so I got out of my car and walked back to the maroon Chevy. It was a warm day. The driver had his window open.

"Find out who I am yet?" I said.

"They're calling me back," the driver said.

I took a business card from my shirt pocket and handed it to him. He read it and nodded, and handed it back to me.

"You know who I am?" he said.

"I know you work for the Templeton Group," I said.

"You got a quicker trace than I did."

"Better contacts," I said. "You want to talk."

"May as well," he said and nodded toward the passenger door. I went around and got in.

"Name's Francis," he said. "Jerry Francis."

He was a square-faced, square-shouldered guy wearing Oakley wraparounds, and a straw fedora with a wide brim and a blue silk hatband.

"Who you tailing?" he said.

"You first," I said.

He shook his head.

"It's against company policy," he said, "to discuss any aspect of a case with any unauthorized person."

"And I'm about as unauthorized as it gets," I said. "On the other hand you showed up a few hundred yards behind Marlene Rowley. That might be a clue."

Francis shrugged.

"I've been tailing Trent Rowley," I said.

Francis grinned.

"Ah, divorce work," he said.

"Who can catch who first," I said.

"And the winner gets most of the assets. You working for her?"

"Yes," I said, "following him."

Francis laughed briefly.

"And you know who I'm working for," he said.

"Him," I said, "following her. You catch her?"

"It's against company policy," Francis said, "to discuss any aspect of a case with unauthorized personnel."

"Of course," I said.

"So far the only person I caught her with was him."

"Her husband?"

"Yeah."

Francis was watching the Rowley house. Through the trees, across the lawn, I could see Marlene Rowley come out of her house. I got out of the car.

Francis started the car.

"Time to go to work," he said.

I closed the door.

Through the window, I said, "Have a nice evening."

"You bet," he said and put the car in drive and moved slowly down toward the corner of the street where Marlene would pull out of her driveway. In a while she did and turned right and after a suitable pause, Francis drove on after her.

I stood on the empty suburban street for a time. I felt left out. I had no one to follow. There was a summer hum of insects, which made everything seem quieter. I listened to the quiet for a bit, then went to my car and started it up. And went home.

Marlene Rowley came to see me in the morning, wearing a yellow summer dress with blue flowers. She sat in a straight chair and crossed her legs, and showed me her kneecaps.

"Did you catch him yet," she said

"Depends what you mean by catch. Want some coffee?"

"No. What have you got?"

"I have him in a hotel room with another woman," I said.

"When?"

"Monday night."

"And you didn't report it?"

"Nope."

"Why not?"

"You feel that being in a hotel room with another woman is enough?" I said.

"No. I want proof. I want the sonovabitch caught with his pants down. Her too. Or them. Or whoever he's screwing."

"Three hours together in a hotel room would probably suffice in divorce court."

"I want it all," she said.

"You want to embarrass him," I said.

"Goddamned right," she said. "Do you have any idea? No. Of course you don't. You couldn't imagine how many dinner parties I ran for his stupid friends. How to make nice chitchat. How many hours at the day spa, so I'd look good. He's cheating on me? Look at me. I'm beautiful. I'm incredibly smart. I've been a perfect wife for him. People like me. They like him, the jerk, because he's married to me. If it weren't for me he'd be running a hardware store someplace. And he cheats on me?"

"Hard to imagine," I said.

"You're damned right. So you stay on him until you've got him cold. I want pictures."

"Pictures," I said.

"Of him and whatever bitch he's fucking."

"In the act," I said.

"Absolutely."

"Should I have them matted and framed?" I said.

"Are you being funny?" she said.

"Apparently not," I said.

"I expect results," she said. "And I expect them promptly. If you can't handle that, I'll find someone who can."

"Why don't you do that," I said.

"What?"

"Why don't you find somebody else to do this work," I said.

"No. Oh my God. No. I didn't mean that. Sometimes I'm so clear on things that I may be too abrupt. I want you. I don't want someone else. I'm sorry. I didn't mean to offend you. I'm sorry."

I put both my hands up, palms toward her. And made a gesture for her to stop.

"I'm not offended," I said.

"I can pay you more," she said.

"My last job, I was paid four donuts," I said. "Your pay scale is fine."

"Then what?"

"I'll make you a deal," I said. "I'll get you evidence sufficient to demonstrate infidelity. And you stop telling me what it is and how to do it."

"I didn't mean to make you mad."

"I'm not mad," I said. "I'm just sort of inner-directed."

Marlene frowned a little and tried to look thoughtful.

"Well," she said. "Can we continue?"

"On my terms," I said.

"Oh, yes, certainly," she said. "That will be fine."

"Okay. I'll stay with your husband for a while, see what else surfaces."

"Thank you," she said.

"Sure."

We sat quietly for a moment. She shifted a little in the chair. She was wearing yellow sling-back heels and no stockings. Her legs were tan. It was May. I suspected artifice.

"I really do like you," she said. "Really."

I nodded.

"Don't you think I'm good-looking?"

"I do," I said.

"I know I frighten a lot of men," she said. "You know—beautiful, educated, rich. Men feel threatened."

"I'm trying to be brave," I said.

"I think you are really good-looking too," she said.

"Guys at the gym are always telling me that," I said.

"It's hard being alone," she said. "And being a woman. I'm counting on you."

"Little lady," I said, "you're in good hands."

"Are you laughing at me?"

"With," I said. "Laughing with."

10

Which was why, later that afternoon, I was back at my post, in line of sight with Trent Rowley's silver Beamer. I had two books with me: Simon Schama's book, *Rembrandt's Eyes*, which was too big to carry around places except when I was doing surveillance in a car. The other was a much smaller book called *Genome*, in case I had to kill time on foot.

The Schama book was not one you read at a sitting, and certainly not at a standing. I'd been reading it a few chapters at a time for several years. I hadn't started *Genome* yet.

People began leaving the Kinergy offices at about 4:30. The Beamer stayed put. I kept reading. At six I started the car up and turned on the radio. The Sox were playing an early evening game for some reason, probably having something to do with television. I was pefectly happy with television, but it always seemed to me that, finally, baseball was designed for radio. The pace of the game gave the announcers time to talk about the game and the players and other players from games past, unless they had so many commercials they had trouble fitting the game around them. By the seventh inning it was too dark to read, even with the interior light on in the car, so I put *Rembrandt* down and listened to the game. By 9:15 the game was over. It was fully dark, and the silver Beamer and I were the only cars left in the lot.

Was Rowley scoring Ellen Eisen in his office? He was the CFO so he must have a couch. I could burst in on him with a camera and shout *ah ha!* But I didn't have a camera, and I had no interest in ever yelling *ah ha!* It would have been especially embarrassing if when I burst in and yelled *ah ha!* he was at his desk going over spreadsheets. Plus, without a camera all I could do when I burst in would be to point my finger at them and say *click.*

I decided not to burst in. I called his office number. His voice mail answered after four rings. I waited another fifteen minutes and called again. Voice mail again. If he'd come out, I wouldn't have missed him. I had been doing this kind of thing too well, for too many years, for me to have missed him. Had he scooted out another door into the waiting arms of Ellen Eisen? Were they even now locked in mad embrace in the back seat of her Volvo station wagon? Or had he been overwhelmed by guilt and slashed his wrists with a Swiss Army knife? I sat in the dark and looked at the encouraging stars and thought about it. I needed to know where he was.

I got out of my car and walked to the glass front door and

knocked. There was a security guy at the desk inside, watching television on a small screen. He picked up the phone and pointed toward me. There was a phone outside the door. I picked it up.

"May I help you?" the security guy said.

"I was supposed to meet Trent Rowley here," I said. "At seven o'clock."

"Your name, sir?"

"Johnny Weismuller," I said.

"I don't see you on our list, Mr. Weisman."

"It was social," I said.

"I don't see how I can help you," the security guy said.

He didn't want to be missing the jackpot question on "Jeopardy."

"I'm getting worried about him," I said. "His car is still here."

"Have you called his office?" the security guy said.

"I have. No answer."

"When Mr. Rowley is working late," the security guy said, "he doesn't like to be disturbed."

And so it went, until I finally said I was going to call the cops.

The security guy heaved a big sigh.

"Wait there," he said. "I'll have someone check."

I waited. He put down my phone and picked up another one and dialed and spoke briefly and hung up and redirected his gaze to the television. I waited. In maybe five minutes the security guy picked up his phone again, and listened, and leaned suddenly back in his chair and looked out at me. Then I saw him nod and break the connection and punch out another number. I saw him wait and then he talked for maybe another two minutes, and hung up. He looked at me again through the glass doorway. Then he picked up the intercom phone and pointed and I picked up my end.

"We are still trying to track Mr. Rowley down, sir. Could I have your name again?"

"Johnny Weismuller," I said and spelled the last name. I wasn't sure how to spell it. Next alias I used would be simpler. Lex Barker, maybe.

"Just hang out there a little longer, sir," he said. "If you would."

"Sure," I said, and hung up and leaned against the outside wall of the entryway.

Something was up and I wanted to know what. In only another minute or two a car pulled into the empty lot, and cruised up and stopped behind me with the headlights pointed at me. It was hard to see in the glare of headlights, but I was pretty sure it was a police cruiser. Two men got out, one from each side, and stood behind the open doors. Through the glare they looked very much like cops. They were cops. It looked like I was the something that was up

"Step over to the car, please," one of the cops said. "Put your hands on the hood."

I did. The cop on the passenger side came around. He had his gun out, holding it down next to his leg pointed at the ground. I put my hands behind my head with my fingers laced.

"He's done this before, Freddie," the cop said.

He holstered his weapon and held my laced hands together with his left hand while he patted me down.

"Gun," I said. "Right hip."

He patted me down anyway, and when he was through, took the gun from the holster and let go of my clasped hands and stepped away from me. I straightened.

"You got some ID?"

"In my wallet."

"Get it out," the cop said.

He was a big kid with freckles and sergeant stripes. I got my wallet out and got out my license to detect and handed it over. He took it and handed it to his partner to read.

"Private detective," the partner said.

He was shorter than his partner, with a narrow face and a low hairline.

"So tell me your story," the first cop said.

Two more cruisers pulled into the parking lot, and behind them an unmarked Ford Crown Vic, with the dead giveaway buggy whip antenna. Unmarked was probably mostly a status symbol. Two guys in plain clothes got out of the Crown Vic and walked toward us. An ambulance pulled into the lot, and behind it a State Police Cruiser.

Big doings at Kinergy.

"This the guy?" one of the plainclothes cops said.

The freckle-faced cop said, "Private eye, Sal."

"Get what you can," Sal said. "We'll talk to him when we come out."

The security guy had the glass door open and Sal and the other detective and four uniforms and two ambulance guys went on into the lobby and up in the elevator.

"So what happened to Rowley?" I said.

"Why you think something happened to Rowley?" Beetle Brow said.

"Just a crazy guess," I said.

Freckles said, "Tell us your story, Mr. Spenser."

I shook my head.

"Not yet," I said.

"We could slap the cuffs on you right now," Beetle Brow said. "Talk to you at the station."

"Am I under arrest?" I said.

"Not yet."

"Then I decline to go."

"You refusing a lawful order, pal?"

I looked at Freckles.

"What is this," I said. "Good cop, stupid cop? I'm not going to tell anybody anything until I have some idea why I'm being asked."

Freckles nodded.

"Freddie," he said. "Whyn't you check around the perimeter of the building, see if there's anything might be useful."

"He call me stupid?" Freddie said.

"No, no," Freckles said. "He was talking about me."

Freddie nodded slowly and gave me a tough look so I wouldn't think I could get away with anything. Then he took a big Mag flashlight from the cruiser and went around the corner of the building.

"According to the call we got," Freckles said, "there's a dead guy on the seventh floor, suspicious circumstances, and you were at the front door asking about him."

"Suspicious circumstances," I said.

Freckles shrugged.

"Our dispatcher talks like that," he said. "You now know what I know. Why were you looking for him."

"I was tailing him for a client," I said. "When he didn't come out, I called his office. When he didn't answer, I wondered and went to the door. Security guard went to check, and that's what I know."

"Who's the client?"

I shook my head.

"You got no privilege here," Freckles said.

"I am an agent of the client's attorney," I said. "His privilege might extend to me."

"I doubt it," Freckles said. "But I'm still in my first year of law school."

"Might work," I said.

"Maybe," Freckles said.

As we were talking another dark Crown Vic pulled into the parking lot. It had the blue plates that Massachusetts puts on official cars.

"Here they are," Freckles said. "State cops."

The car door opened and Healy got out.

I said, "Evening, Captain."

He looked at me for a moment.

"Oh shit," he said.

"Oh shit?"

"Yeah. You're in this."

"So?"

"So that means it'll be a fucking mess."

"I thought you'd welcome my help," I said.

"Like a case of clap," Healy said.

"That's cold," I said.

"It is," Healy said and walked on past me toward the Kinergy Building.

"You know the captain," Freckles said.

"I do," I said. "We're tight."

"I could see that," Freckles said.

11

It was 5:30 in the morning. Healy and I were drinking coffee out of thick white mugs at the counter of a small diner on Route 20. I felt the way you feel when you've been up all night and drunk too much coffee. If I still smoked, I would have drunk too much coffee and smoked too many cigarettes and felt worse. It wasn't much in the way of consolation. But one makes do.

"Good aim?" I said.

"Or good luck," Healy said. "Any one of the three shots would have been enough. ME thinks he was dead three, four hours."

"That would make it about six or seven in the evening."

"Yep."

"Lotta people still in the building at that time."

"Yep."

"Widens the range of suspects," I said.

"Yep. Anybody coulda done it. Anybody still working. Anybody walked in during business hours, hung around afterwards."

"So, basically, anyone could have shot him," I said.

"We'll start by talking with everyone who worked after five," Healy said.

"Security?" I said.

"Sign-in starts at five. There's a guard on the front desk and a roamer in the building. We're checking anybody signed in, make sure all the names match."

"Why would you wait until after five and sign in," I said, "when you could go in at five of five and not sign in."

"You wouldn't," Healy said.

"But procedure is procedure," I said.

"Un-huh."

"Why I left the cops," I said.

"You left the cops because they canned your ass for being an insubordinate fucking hot dog," Healy said.

"Well, yeah," I said. "That too."

The plump blond woman behind the counter poured more coffee into my mug. I didn't need more. I didn't want more. But there it was. I stirred in some sugar.

"Hard," I said, "to fire off three rounds in a still-populated office building and nobody hears it."

"We don't yet know if anyone did," Healy said. "We'll start canvassing this morning."

"But no one reported any gunshots," I said.

"Nope."

"On the other hand," I said "people don't report gunfire anyway."

"Only in areas where they recognize it," Healy said, "and half expect to hear it."

"People like these," I said. "They hear bang bang and they don't call for fear that it'll turn out to be some guy with a power nailer fixing something in the third-floor men's room, and they'll look like an asshole."

"For most of these folks," Healy said, "it's probably too late to worry about looking like an asshole."

"Ah, Captain," I said. "A life of crime-busting has made you cynical. What kind of gun?"

"They haven't dug the slugs out yet. Looking at the holes I'd say a nine."

"Silencer?"

"Don't know yet," Healy said. "Whoever did it had large balls. You and I both know silencers will cut down sound, but they won't prevent it. Our shooter walks in, pops the guy, walks out. People in the hallways, people in the elevators."

"Probably took him, what, a minute?"

"He only needed balls for a little while," he said. "But for that little while he needed a lot of them."

I was looking at our server behind the counter. She had on a cropped white tee shirt and constrictive jeans that hung low enough on her hips to display the blue butterfly tattooed at the base of her spine.

"So why were you tailing this guy?"

I drank some coffee and didn't say anything.

"You know," Healy said, "and I know, that the reason you're

tailing him may suggest a motive for murder. Might point us somewhere."

I nodded.

"You know anything that will point us anywhere?"

"Do I ever," I said.

Healy's eggs arrived and he ate some.

"His wife," I said, "hired me to get the goods on him for a divorce."

"Did you?"

"Yeah, he's cheating on her, but I don't have pictures."

"Pictures," Healy said.

"Yeah. She insists on pictures. In the act."

"Jealous wife ain't a bad motive," Healy said.

I didn't tell him about Elmer O'Neill. Or the Eisens. I saw nothing useful to me for the moment to say anything about the guy Rowley hired to follow his wife. She was after all a client and I might as well protect her as far as I could. I could always tell it later. For the moment holding it back might give me a useful thing to trade someday. I had never gotten into serious trouble keeping my yap shut.

"What we can be pretty sure of," I said, "is whoever wanted him dead, wanted him dead pretty bad. Walk in and shoot him, no attempt to make it look like an accident, or a suicide. They wanted it done quick."

Healy bit the corner off a triangle of toast and chewed it slowly and swallowed.

"Or they were so mad it didn't matter to them," Healy said.

"That narrows it down," I said.

Healy grinned at me.

"Yeah, it was either a crime of passion or it wasn't," he said.

12

Marlene and I discussed her husband's death, sitting on the side porch, sipping iced tea and looking at the uneventful sweep of her front lawn.

"A person from the state police called me," Marlene said. "A captain."

"Healy," I said.

"Whatever," she said. "Did you get the pictures of Trent cheating?"

"No."

"I told you I wanted pictures."

I nodded.

"Have you identified the woman?" Marlene said.

"Does it matter now?" I said.

"Of course it matters," Marlene said. "I'm paying for this in-formation."

"Woman's name is Ellen Eisen."

"My God," she said, "that stupid little Jew."

"Nicely said."

"Oh, God. Don't get *PC* on me. She *is* a stupid little Jew."

There didn't seem anywhere to take that, so I nodded and left it.

"Sorry things worked out the way they did," I said.

"Don't worry about me. I'm strong. I can take it. I don't need any sympathy."

"I'm sorry anyway," I said.

"They'll think I did it," Marlene said.

"They will?"

"Of course they will, they always suspect the wife."

"In a homicide," I said, "the cops routinely investigate every-body. They'll clear you."

"My friends will think I did it. I know they will. They will love blaming me."

"What are friends for?" I said.

She paid no attention.

"They'll think because of who I am, the police would be in-timidated and not really investigate."

The image of her intimidating Healy made me smile, but Marlene took no notice.

"I'll need you to prove I wasn't involved," she said.

"I don't think you do," I said. "On the reasonable assump-tion that you weren't, I should think the cops could do that on their own."

"You still work for me," she said. "I want to be cleared."

"Where were you last night," I said, "between, say, six and ten."

"I went to the movies."

"Where?"

"At that new big theater complex near the new Ritz."

"What did you see?"

"*Chicago.* And I don't like being questioned this way."

"The easiest way to be cleared is to have an alibi," I said.

"Well, I was at the movies. I often go into Boston alone to the movies."

"You didn't see anyone you knew?"

"No."

"You have the ticket stub?"

"No, of course not, why would I save a ticket stub?"

I was quiet.

"It's like you think I did do it," she said.

"You have very little chance of getting at the truth," I said, "if you know in advance what the truth ought to be."

"Oh don't lecture me," she said. "Go do your job."

"Marlene," I said. "I think I'm going to have to file you under Life's Too Short."

"Excuse me?"

"I quit again."

She stared at me.

"You can't quit," she said.

"Sure I can."

I stood up.

"I'll send my bill to Randy," I said.

She began to cry. I started for the door. She cried harder.

"Please," she said.

I got to the door.

"Please," she said again.

I looked back. She was bent way over in her chair as if her stomach hurt. Her face was buried in her hands.

"Please don't leave," she said. "Please don't leave me like this."

She had me. I put my hand on the doorknob but I knew I wasn't going to turn it. I took in some air. She blubbered.

"Okay," I said.

"What?"

"Okay," I said.

I turned away from the door and went back and sat down. I was 0 for 2, quitting.

13

Dr. Silverman and I looked at the Gainsborough exhibit all morning at the Museum of Fine Arts. Then we went for lunch in the museum restaurant. Susan had salad. I had fruit and cheese. We shared a bottle of pinot grigio.

"I doubt that she was faking the hysterics," Susan said to me. "It is not easy to do."

"You ever do it?"

"No."

"Even when I propose sex?"

"Those are real hysterics," Susan said.

I ate a seedless grape.

"Funny thing," I said. "She didn't get hysterical over her husband's death."

"They were estranged, after all," Susan said.

"First thing she wanted to know was if he was cheating, and did I get pictures."

Susan took a bite from a leaf of Boston lettuce.

"Was he?" she said.

"Yes, I had him in a hotel room for several hours with a woman."

"You told her."

"Yeah. That's what she hired me for."

"Maybe."

"Maybe?"

"Pictures?" Susan said.

"No. I probably was never going to get the pictures she wanted."

"Because?"

"Because she wanted them *en flagrante.*"

"And you found it repellent to get such pictures."

"I did."

"And why did she want such pictures?" Susan said.

Susan had forgotten her salad.

"Said she wanted rock solid proof when she went into divorce court," I said.

Susan nodded slowly. She was in her focused mode. In her focused mode she could set things on fire.

"Divorces are often granted without such evidence," she said.

"Usually," I said.

Susan sipped her wine, and was silent. She would often stop like that, in the middle of a discussion, when she had come across something interesting. I knew she was thinking about it. I waited.

"It's a way to be part of it," Susan said.

"Part of . . . ?"

"The partner of someone who is having an adulterous affair is excluded. Seeing pictures, having information, is a way of not being excluded, of becoming, so to speak, a part of the action."

"Knowledge is power?" I said.

"Knowledge is participation," Susan said. "A way not to be left out. And, probably, a sort of revenge."

"Because it would humiliate him to be caught on camera?"

"His every secret revealed," Susan said.

"You think that's why she hired me?"

"Things are never one thing," Susan said. "There are always several truths."

"So," I said. "She wanted to clean his clock in the divorce. She wanted revenge. And she what . . . something else?"

"Well," Susan said. "She would be a third participant in a covert sexual liaison."

"So she'd get sexual pleasure."

"Yep."

"Voyeurism?"

"Well, sure, I suppose. If you define voyeurism as getting pleasure out of observing sex."

"That would cover a pretty good segment of the population," I said.

"I seem to recall somebody peeking in the mirrors on a hotel room wall once?"

"Voyeurism," I said.

"Which is why, Mirror Boy, putting a name to behavior doesn't always add much information."

"Will this be on the midterm?" I said.

She smiled.

"God," she said, "I do lecture, don't I."

"And beautifully," I said.

"Is she a suspect?" Susan said.

"Marlene? In her husband's murder? No more than the husband's girlfriend, or the husband's girlfriend's husband, or the wife of the guy Marlene was seeing if she was seeing anybody, or the guy Marlene was seeing if she was seeing anybody."

"Wow!"

"A serial gang bang," I said. "Maybe."

"So hiring you to clear her name seems a little premature."

"It's not the cops," I said. "It's her friends."

"How lovely," Susan said.

"You think in fact it's really the continuing quest for, ah, voyeuristic information?"

"Yes."

"Even though he's dead?"

"Yes," Susan said. "He won't escape her that easily."

"What do you think about her own affair?"

"If there really was one, I'd guess it was a case of revenge fuck."

"That a Freudian expression?" I said.

"Actually," Susan said. "I believe I learned it from you."

"Glad you've been paying attention," I said.

"And, of course you have agreed to continue."

"Well, the pay is good, and she did cry—you know how I hate crying—and I'm sort of curious about who killed her husband while I was outside watching."

Susan smiled.

"What?" I said.

"Even if the pay were bad and she didn't cry," Susan said.

"You think I'd do it just because I'm curious?"

"Without question," Susan said.

"You shrinks think you know everything," I said.

"Am I right?" Susan said.

"Yes."

14

Between Washington Street and Tremont, near the Boylston Street corner, in what publicists were trying to call the Ladder District, a second Ritz Carlton Hotel had been built in the same redevelopment effort that produced the movie theater complex where Marlene said she had seen *Chicago*. Associated with the hotel was a passel of high-end condominiums, in one of which, on the top floor, Ellen and Bernard Eisen lived in maybe less harmony than they had once hoped. Ellen was expecting me.

When I had seen her the other night, coming out of the Hyatt Hotel with Trent Rowley, I had noted in a professional sort of way that she was a semi-knockout. But seeing her in the bright morning light I decided to upgrade her knockout-ness to full. In tight maroon sweats, her legs didn't seem heavy after all. Just strong.

"Let's sit in the living room," she said. "There's a nice view of the Common."

I followed her down a small corridor and into a big bright room with wall-to-wall carpet and big windows through which there was in fact a nice view of the Common. And the Public Gardens. And the Charles River Basin. And Cambridge. And, maybe, on a clear day, eternity. The room had been organized around the view. There was a big beige couch facing the window, and two big tan leather high-backed wing chairs, kitty-corner to the window so that the occupant could look at the view and still talk with someone on the couch. Seated in perfect repose in one of the chairs was a man with dark, very big, very deep-set eyes. He was a slender guy with a short gray beard. His hair was gray, and what was left was wavy and long in the back. His high forehead was nicely tanned.

He rose from the chair effortlessly when Ellen Eisen introduced us. Standing he was maybe two inches taller than I was. Which made him tall. His name, she said, was Darrin O'Mara. We shook hands. His handshake, for all the near theatricality of his appearance and movements, was soft. His deep-eyed gaze was direct and sort of reassuring. When he spoke I heard a faint lilt. Irish maybe.

"Pleasure to meet you," he said.

"What can we do for you, Mr. Spenser," Ellen said.

O'Mara sat back down and crossed his legs effortlessly. His freshly creased slacks were the color of butterscotch. His wing-tipped loafers were burgundy. He wore no socks. He had on a starched white shirt, open at the throat, and a blue blazer with brass buttons. My clothes must never fit that well, I thought. I'd be overwhelmed with sexual opportunities, and never get any work done. I promised myself to be careful.

"I have sort of a delicate matter to discuss," I said.

"You may speak freely in front of Darrin," Ellen said.

"Are you her lawyer?" I said to Darrin.

He smiled gently. I thought maybe I'd seen him someplace before.

"Oh, God, no," Ellen said. "I hate lawyers. Darrin is my advisor. I asked him to be here."

"This isn't a financial thing," I said.

"I'm an advisor in matters of the heart," Darrin said in his soft lilt.

It was the matters-of-the-heart phrase that made me remember him. He had a local talk show called "Matters of the Heart." It was a call-in radio talk show from seven to midnight three nights a week. In the last year or so one of the local stations had begun to televise the radio show live.

"Ah yes," I said. "That Darrin O'Mara."

He put his fingertips together and put them to his mouth and smiled modestly. Ellen looked at him as if he had just strolled in across the harbor.

"As I mentioned," I said to her, "I'm looking into the death of Trent Rowley."

"Yes."

"You knew Mr. Rowley?"

"Yes. He and my husband worked together."

I looked at O'Mara. He smiled at me sweetly over his fingertips. I thought a little.

"I have no secrets from Darrin," Ellen said.

I nodded.

"Okay," I said. "I know you and Trent Rowley were intimate."

She stared at me calmly. O'Mara continued to give me the benign eyeball.

"How do you know that?" Ellen said.

"Reasonable supposition," I said. "I tailed him to the Hyatt in Cambridge last week. You and he were in room seven-seventeen together for about three hours."

"And you choose to give that fact the most lurid interpretation possible."

"I do."

She looked at O'Mara.

Speaking softly, he said, "Trust the truth, Ellie, remember?"

She looked into his eyes for a little while.

"There is no deceit involved," she said. "My husband and I have an open marriage."

O'Mara looked proud.

"And your husband is aware of that," I said.

"Oh, don't be small-minded. It is very unbecoming."

"So he didn't object to you spending time with Trent Rowley."

"No. Of course not."

O'Mara spoke in his deep gentle voice.

"Are you familiar, Mr. Spenser, with the ancient tradition of courtly love?"

"Love is available only without the coercion of marriage?" I said.

O'Mara hadn't expected me to know. He was far too deeply centered to blink, but he did pause for a moment.

"Only in circumstances where love is unbidden by law or convention can it truly be given and received."

"That too," I said.

"In my work I apply the courtly love tradition to contemporary marriage. Only when a wife is free to choose another can she be free to choose her husband."

"Heady," I said. "Do you have any idea why someone would wish to shoot Trent Rowley?"

"Lord, no," Ellen said.

"Enlightened as he is about courtly love," I said, "your husband wouldn't put several jealous slugs into Rowley's head, would he?"

"Don't be coarse," she said.

"He did hire a guy named Elmer O'Neill to follow you around," I said. I had no idea where I was going. I was just poking into the anthill to see if any ants came out.

"Excuse me?"

"Elmer O'Neill, private eye. We met at the Hyatt, me tailing Rowley, Elmer tailing you."

"That can't be true," Ellen said,. "My husband and I have traveled far beyond the petty constraints of jealousy."

"Then why would he have you followed?" I said.

She looked at O'Mara. He nodded gently.

"It seems apparent," he said, "that Ellen cannot attest to the truth of your allegation."

"I wasn't asking her to," I said. "I was asking her why she thought her husband might do it."

"A quibble," O'Mara said. "I believe we are through with this interview."

"That so, Mrs. Eisen?"

She looked at O'Mara again. He nodded gently again.

"Yes," she said. "Please go."

There was a small schoolyard impulse, a vestige of my more heedless youth, that made me want to say *no*, and see what O'Mara did. But it wouldn't take me anywhere useful, so I nodded pleasantly instead.

"Thanks for your time," I said.

"What are you going to do?" she said.

"I'll be traveling beyond the petty constraints of rejection," I said.

15

I went over to Kinergy to talk with Bernie Eisen. The security guy at the front desk took my name and made a phone call, and in a minute or two a shiny bright guy with short hair and rimless glasses appeared. His hair was so blond it was nearly white. His suit and shirt were banker gray, with a silver tie. Everything was ironed and starched and pressed and fitted. His cropped mustache was perfectly trimmed. His black wing tips gleamed with polish. His nails were manicured. He had small eyes magnified by the glasses.

"Mr. Spenser? Gavin, director of security."

He put out his hand. We shook. His grip was everything it should have been. I went easy, so as not to frighten him.

"I wonder if you could step on into my office, for just a couple of minutes," Gavin said.

"Sure," I said.

Number six on the Spenser Crime Stoppers List is, go with the flow. We took the elevator to the top of the building, and walked down a bright corridor to Gavin's big office. There were three slick-looking secretaries in the outer office, all wearing skirts, and all smelling faintly of good perfume. They seemed busy. Two on computers, one on the phone.

We sat in Gavin's private office. It was almost empty. Desk, three straight chairs, a file cabinet. The walls were white. There were no pictures. The floor was darkly polished hardwood, no rugs. The only thing on Gavin's desk was a big white telephone with a lot of buttons.

"I hope you understand," Gavin said. "We've had a terrible event just this week here, and we're trying to, ah, screen anyone who comes to see our executives."

"Of course," I said.

"Why did you want to see Mr. Eisen?" Gavin said.

"Personal," I said. "I'm not sure Eisen would want me to share it."

"Now, you're not going to give me trouble, are you?" Gavin said.

"Not if you don't annoy me," I said.

"Do I annoy you?"

"Not yet," I said.

"Perhaps," Gavin said, "we could ask Mr. Eisen to come in and help us work things."

"Sure," I said.

Gavin spoke to one of the secretaries on an intercom. While

we were waiting I looked at the room some more. It was on a corner, with big windows on two sides. There were no draperies. It wasn't Gavin's fault that the windows didn't look out on much. A view of the parking lot from one, a glimpse of Route 128 from another.

"Coffee?" Gavin said as we waited.

I said yes. He spoke again into the intercom, and in a little while the coffee came in big mugs with the Kinergy logo. The secretary who brought the coffee had bountiful dark hair and very good legs. I thought she might have looked at me speculatively, but she might have simply been evaluating me as a security risk. Eisen came into Gavin's office right after the leggy secretary left. He was carrying his own coffee in a mug that said "Bernz" on it.

"Bernie Eisen," he said when he came in.

He gave me a manly little handshake.

"Mr. Spenser says he has something of a personal nature to discuss with you, Bernz," Gavin said. "In the light of the recent tragedy, I thought maybe we ought to sit in."

"That's great, Gav," Bernie said.

He looked at me.

"I don't mean to be too direct," he said, "but who are you?"

"I'm a detective," I said. "Investigating the death of Trent Rowley."

"I already talked to a detective named Healy."

"He's state," I said. "I'm private."

Bernie frowned. He was a short guy, with sharp features. His black hair was slicked back. His black silk suit looked as if it may have cost more than my entire wardrobe, including my lizard-skin ammo belt. He had on a gray shirt with no tie, and managed to achieve both professional and relaxed, which was very likely what he wanted to achieve. He looked like a guy who worked out regularly with his personal trainer.

"Employed by whom?" Gavin said.

"You knew," I said to Eisen, "about your wife's relationship to Rowley."

"Hold it right there," Gavin said.

His jaw was hard set. His face was suddenly angular. His little eyes got even smaller. Eisen immediately had the same look.

"You should know," I said. "You hired a guy to follow her."

"Don't answer that," Gavin said.

I said, "Would you prefer to talk somewhere else, Mr. Eisen?"

"He would not," Gavin said. "This conversation is over."

"Mr. Eisen?" I said.

"I have nothing to say," Eisen said. He was giving me as tough a look as a guy his size could give.

"And I'll have to ask you to leave," Gavin said to me.

It wasn't going to go well here. I thought about bouncing Gavin on his crew cut for a while, but decided that it would be self-indulgent.

"Have a lovely day," I said, and turned, and went.

16

Susan and I spent Saturday morning together in a series of flossy little stores on Newbury Street, where all the clerks knew her and called her Mrs. Silverman, except for a few of the most seriously expensive, where they called her Susan. Twice I was offered Perrier, but otherwise, they ignored me. Which was fine with me. If the store had someplace to sit, and most of the stores did, I didn't mind shopping with Susan. I liked to watch her with the clothes. I liked to watch her interact with the clerks. I liked it when she'd come out of the dressing room and model something. I liked it that she cared what I thought. I liked it that she wanted my company. I took a proprietary pleasure when she'd invite me to consult at the dressing room door, where she was half clothed. The fact that in most of the stores I fit in like a warthog at a cat show did not dampen my spirits.

For lunch we went to the refurbished Ritz Café. This was the original Ritz, not the new one where the Eisens had their condo. It had been spruced and polished and modified, but the windows in the café still gave out onto Newbury Street. We got a seat in the window bay and watched the cold spring rain.

"Why do you suppose that security man was so icky?" Susan said.

"Part of it would probably be—what do you shrinkos call it?—characterological," I said.

"Shrinkos," Susan said. "How sweet."

"And some of it, I don't know. He clearly didn't want Eisen to answer me."

"Do you think he'll talk to you at home, or somewhere away from Gavin?"

"Eisen seems eager to be a winner, not a loser, and I'd guess that he got a firm lecture from Gavin on how loose lips sink ships."

"So he won't?"

"Probably not. Unless there's something scares him more than Gavin."

"Is Gavin really that scary?"

"He seems a nasty guy," I said. "Rigid, anal, mean, spends too much time on his appearance."

"That last is not always a fault," Susan said.

"As we've just recently proved," I said. "But you aside. This guy looks like he's assembled by a drill team every morning."

"In many firms the chief of security is a middle-management functionary," Susan said.

"I know," I said. "You ever hear of a guy named Darrin O'Mara?"

Susan laughed.

"The radio guy?"

"Yeah. What do you think of him professionally?"

"Darrin O'Mara?" Susan laughed again and flapped her hands as she searched for the right phrase. "He's a . . . he's a talk show host."

"He make any sense?"

"No, of course not. He looks good and he has a nice voice, and his show has a catchy title."

" 'Matters of the Heart,' " I said.

"Yes," Susan said. "And I listen to it sometimes, because some of my less worldly patients listen to him."

"So do I hear you saying you don't hold with courtly love?" I said.

"Courtly love is a poetic conceit," Susan said. "You know that."

"We're not married," I said.

"That's true. And it's true that we love each other. And it has nothing to do with the conventions of Provençal poetry. We haven't married because the two of us have autonomy needs that marriage doesn't serve."

"Gee," I said. "Not so we'd be free to love uncoerced?"

"You know that we'd love each other married or unmarried. But we are probably happier—though neither more nor less in love—unmarried."

"So you are not one to promote adultery."

"It is the most destructive act in a relationship," Susan said. "You know all this perfectly well. You just like me to talk about us."

"I do," I said.

17

After lunch, Susan went home to shuffle her new clothes around, and I went down to 100 Summer Street to visit the Templeton Group, which was a small office in a big building. There were two desks in the office, and a client chair and a telephone. Jerry Francis was at one of the desks. No one was at the other.

"Not the biggest group I ever saw," I said when I went in.

Francis remembered me.

"Hey," he said. "There's another guy here, too."

"Templeton?" I said.

"There is no Templeton," Francis said. "My partner's name is Bellini. We thought Templeton Group sounded good with the address."

"Nothing is as it appears," I said. "I'm looking for a little help. Gumshoe to gumshoe."

"I'm starting to choke up," Francis said. "Whaddya want?"

"What can you tell me about Marlene Rowley? Or her husband?"

"It's against company policy . . ." Francis said.

I said the rest of it with him. ". . . to discuss any aspect of a case with any unauthorized person."

"Fast learner," Francis said.

"Yeah. I was hoping for collegial cooperation here," I said. "But I see that's not forthcoming. Lemme try another approach. Your client was murdered. I have made no mention of you to the investigating officers."

"And if I stand firm on company policy?" Francis said.

"Then the cops will be asking you."

"You'd rat me out to the cops."

"Well put," I said.

"What happened to collegiality?" Francis said.

"Outmoded concept," I said. "Tell me about Marlene and Trent."

He wasn't wearing his fancy sunglasses inside, and it left his eyes looking sort of vulnerable. He leaned back in his chair and put his feet up on the desk and clasped his hands behind his head.

"Nice names," he said. "Marlene and Trent. It's like they were born to be yuppies."

"Just fulfilling their destiny," I said.

"So this guy Trent Rowley comes in to see us, says he thinks his wife is fooling around on him, wants her followed."

"Did he say how he came to you?"

"No, and we didn't ask."

"The cash up front made a good bona fide."

"It did," Francis said. "So Mario—Bellini, my partner—
Mario asks him is he looking for divorce evidence. You know?
It's one thing to see her with some other guy. It's another thing
if they get into court."

I nodded.

"He says he wants to know everyone she sees," Francis said.
"Men, women, everybody. I think to myself, what is she, an
equal opportunity cheater? But I don't say nothing because we
ain't doing so well we can be messing with prospective clients,
you know?"

"Maybe you should downgrade the location," I said.

"Impresses the clients," he said.

"So you tailed her," I said.

"Yep, two shifts, sixteen hours a day. Mario took one, I took
the other. We figured she had to sleep eight hours."

"Get a third partner," I said. "You can offer twenty-four-
hour service."

"Then we could get that eye, you know, says *we never sleep?*"

"I think somebody already used that," I said. "What did you
observe?"

"Observe? Whoa, you can really talk."

"I know a woman with a Ph.D.," I said.

"She hot?"

"Yes. What did you see?"

"Marlene ain't got much of a life," Francis said. "She goes to
the market couple times a week. Goes to the hairdresser on

Wednesdays. Has a personal trainer come in three times a week. Went to a play at that theater near Harvard Square Friday night."

"The American Repertory Theater," I said.

"Whatever," Francis said. "Thing is, she went alone. She goes every place alone. In the time we been tailing her I never seen her with anyone except her trainer, and Mario says he ain't either."

"Trainer a man or woman?"

"Man."

"Get a name?"

"Sure, traced his tags. Name's Mark Silver. Lives in Gloucester."

"She go places with her husband?" I said.

"I never saw him except that once. Maybe he came home after eleven at night when we wasn't on the clock."

"Weekends?"

"Never seen him."

"So you call him at work to report."

"Nope. He calls us. I don't even know where he works."

"So where do you send the bill?" I said.

"Don't," Francis said. "He come in every Friday and paid us for the week ahead."

"Check?"

"Cash."

"Doesn't that seem a little funny to you?"

"Sure," Francis said, "but it was a lot of cash."

"Why would a guy have you tail his wife and go to so much trouble to conceal his identity?" I said.

"Figured we could always find him if we had to," Francis said. "We got his home address."

"Maybe," I said.

Francis was still sitting tilted back, hands behind his head. He remained in that position for another moment then slowly picked his feet up and put them on the ground. The chair tilted forward. He unlaced his hands and put them palms down on his desktop and drummed his fingertips lightly.

"You think it ain't him?" Francis said.

"You ever see them together?"

"Just that one time."

"What's he look like?"

"Medium-size blond guy," Francis said. "Very blond, little mustache. Rimless glasses. Looks in shape."

I nodded.

"Yeah," I said. "Sounds like him."

18

I went to see Elmer O'Neill at his office in a converted gas station in Arlington. The gas pumps were gone, but the low concrete pedestal on which they'd once sat was still there.

"I see what you mean about low overhead," I said when I went in.

"Overhead any lower," Elmer said, "and I couldn't stand up straight."

"Right in the heart of the action, too," I said.

"Whaddya need?" Elmer said.

"Bernard Eisen," I said. "What'd he look like?"

"Guy hired me to tail his wife?"

"Yep."

"Blond guy, little mustache, glasses."

"How'd he pay you?"

Elmer squinted at me.

"What's goin' on?" he said.

"Just confirming a few loose ends," I said.

"The hell you are," Elmer said. "Why do you want to know how he paid me?"

I grinned.

"Hard to throw one past you," I said.

"Don't forget it."

"He pay you cash?" I said.

"Why do you want to know?"

"Bernie has a history of bad checks," I said. "Just wondered if he bounced one on you."

"Hell no," Elmer said. "Nobody's bouncing nothing on Elmer O'Neill."

"So his check was good?"

"Better than that," Elmer said proudly. "He paid cash. Up front."

"Cash don't bounce," I said.

"You got that right," Elmer said.

"And what, exactly, did he want?"

"Follow the wife. Tell him who she saw."

"Even another woman?"

"He wanted a full report." Elmer smiled. "Men, women, you know it could go either way."

"Elmer, you sophisticated devil," I said.

"Hey," Elmer said. "It happens."

"Yes it does," I said. "You have any help?"

"Me? No. I don't see no reason to split a fee when all I got to do is work hard, and get it all."

"So you covered her day and night?"

"Picked her up in the morning, stayed with her until bed-time. Bedtime at home."

I nodded.

"Now," I said. "I'm going to take a guess, and you tell me if the guess is on the money or not."

"Yeah?"

"To make sure nobody got wind of it, you didn't report. He called you."

"Yeah, that's right."

"No phone number."

"No."

"Nothing in writing."

"No."

"That raise any flags for you?" I said.

"It did," he said. "It sent up a big flag that said, Elmer, you take that cash right down to the bank and deposit it in your account."

"How'd he happen to come to you?" I said.

"He wanted the best," Elmer said.

"But how'd he find that out," I said.

Elmer squinted at me again.

"There's something going on," he said. "What is it? What's going down?"

I thought about it.

"Same guy who hired you to follow Ellen Eisen hired some-body else to follow another woman."

"Maybe old Bernie's got a . . ."

Elmer stopped. He rocked back in his chair and pointed a forefinger which he jabbed at me gently.

"Old Bernie ain't old Bernie," he said.

I nodded.

"So who the fuck is he?" Elmer said.

"Don't know," I said.

"Then why'd you ask me to describe my guy?" Elmer said.

"Because I've seen Bernie."

"He tell the other guy that he was that woman's husband?"

"Yes."

"And you seen her husband too," Elmer said.

"Yes."

Elmer sat some more, squinting. He still had his forefinger extended but now he was slowly making circles with it in the air. You could sort of track his thinking with it. The closer he got to an idea, the smaller the circles.

"This has got something to do with that company," he said.

"You think?"

"Kinergy," he said. "Guy got killed out there."

"You don't miss much," I said.

"Can't. Not in this business. You involved?"

"I didn't do it," I said.

"You got a piece of the investigation?"

"I'm a curious guy," I said.

"You do have a piece," Elmer said. "You need any help on it, you let me know. Surveillance. Research."

He reached out and patted the computer on his desktop.

"I can surf that fucking Internet," he said. "I can find out a lot."

"Got no budget for you," I said.

"That could change," Elmer said. "There's a lot of money floating around over there."

"At Kinergy?"

"Yeah. Stock almost doubled last year in a bear market," Elmer said. "Anything you need? You know? Be nice to get a foot in that door."

I thanked Elmer for his help and promised that I wouldn't forget him, which was probably true. We shook hands. Elmer walked me three steps to the door. We shook hands again. And I left.

19

Pearl and I ran from the Hatch Shell up to the BU Bridge and back. We were sitting now together on a bench near the Shell looking at the river. I was getting my breathing back under control. Pearl, as far as I could tell, had not elevated her heart rate. A young woman with good gluteus maximus was stretching her hamstrings at the next bench. As she did she looked at Pearl and smiled.

When she finished stretching she straightened and said, "May I pat?"

"Sure," I said. "Either one of us."

The young woman smiled and scratched Pearl behind her left ear.

"Weimaraner," she said. "Right?"

"German shorthaired pointer," I said.

"You sure?" the young woman said.

"Pretty sure," I said.

"How old?"

"Two."

"What's her name?"

"Pearl," I said.

"How'd you train her to sit like that?" the young woman said.

"She likes to sit like that."

The young woman smiled vaguely, said, "Goodbye, Pearl," and jogged off.

"Great way to meet chicks," I said to Pearl.

She leaned over and gave me a large slobber near my nose. I wiped my face with my sleeve. What had begun as a no-brainer of a divorce tail was showing every sign of turning into a hairball. Marlene had hired me. But apparently Francis and O'Neill had been hired under false pretenses, by Gavin the security guy. Why did he want a tail on Marlene Rowley and Ellen Eisen? Did he care who they were sleeping with? If they were sleeping with? He wanted a report on everyone they saw. That sounded like more than an adultery issue.

Pearl spotted two ducks floating in the water fifty feet off shore. Her body tensed. She began to quiver. But she stayed where she was, sitting on the bench beside me.

"Can't bear to leave me," I said. "Can you."

She gave me another big slobber on my face that could have meant *yes,* but could have meant *no* just as easily. The two ducks flew off. Pearl watched them go.

No wonder Bernie Eisen had been confused when I'd brought

up the tail on Mrs. Eisen. And no wonder Gavin had cut it short. Why had Gavin used private guys rather than his own people? Obviously, he didn't want it known. Why had he used these two minor leaguers for the job? Because they would need the money bad enough not to question the cash-only arrangement, where they had no phone or address for him. What was he after? He was the director of security for a major company. But if he was acting on behalf of his employer, he was certainly being covert about it.

On the other hand, if he wasn't, where was the money coming from? The Templeton Group might work cheap, and Elmer O'Neill might work cheap, but even cheap, eighteen hours a day, each, is a lot of cash. Security directors, even big leaguers like Gavin, normally didn't make that kind of money. I looked at Pearl, who was still watching the river, alert to any possibility that the ducks might return.

"So, suppose he is working for the company," I said.

She shifted her big gold-colored eyes at me for a minute, and then went back to the duck watch. What would the company be after with these women, and why would they want to keep it quiet? Most companies would probably try to cover up the fact that they had surveillance on employees' wives. It would not make recruiting any easier if word got around that your spouse might be spied on. On the other hand in these two cases there was actually hanky-panky going on. I didn't know yet if Marlene had been cheating on Trent. But I knew he'd been cheating on her. And I knew Ellen Eisen had been cheating on Bernie—if cheating was possible in an open marriage. I'd have to check that with Darrin O'Mara.

Maybe there were more than these two instances. Maybe it

was company policy. But if surveillance was a policy, it might still be covert, but it would be better organized than handing wads of cash under the table to two second-rate gumshoes, and calling them up for a report. There were too many employees. This deal was a seat-of-the-pants operation.

A squirrel dashed past us. Without hesitating, Pearl was off the bench and after him. The squirrel barely made the tree, and barely got up it before Pearl was standing on her hind legs at the base.

Francis and O'Neill were certainly through. Trent's death blew that cover, and what I'd said to Eisen in front of Gavin had ended it for O'Neill. It would be easy enough to find out if Gavin put a new tail on the women. Same way I had before. But that wouldn't tell me why. What was required was a brilliant stroke of detection. I couldn't think of one. The best I could do was go around and talk to the same people again. If you keep poking, something will eventually come buzzing out. I went to get Pearl, still on her back legs, staring up the tree. I didn't have to bend over to put her leash on.

My friend Ms. Gluteus appeared, returning from her run. I watched her as she came toward us. Expensive shoes. Black tights, loose tee shirt, headband. She wore a curved yellow radio on her arm, the small earphones in place. In her left hand she carried a water bottle with one of those nozzles that allow you to squirt the water in without breaking stride. About twenty-four yards away she slowed to a walk and when she reached the tree where Pearl had cornered the prey, she stopped, breathing hard, and patted Pearl again.

"What kind did you say?"

"German shorthaired squirrel hound," I said.

"Not a weimaraner?"

"No."

"I also thought she might be a chocolate Lab."

"No."

I could tell she was skeptical, but I seemed so sure. So after another couple of pats, she smiled and walked away drinking water from her squirt bottle.

20

I was back in the Eisens' flossy new condo looking at the view again, and drinking a light scotch and soda. Ellen and Bernie were having martinis that Ellen had made while we men got comfortable. Sadly, Darrin couldn't join us.

"I don't know what to tell you, Spenser," Eisen was saying. "I simply did not hire anyone to follow Ellen."

I was particularly fond of people who barely knew me calling me by my last name.

"Well, Eisen," I said. "Somebody was following her."

"That's ridiculous," Eisen said.

"It is," I said. "But there you have it."

"Honestly, Mr. Spenser," Ellen said. "I don't believe anyone was following me."

I smiled at her.

"You got it wrong, pal," Eisen said.

I was even more fond of people who called me pal. I tried to remain focused.

"How about Gavin?" I said.

"Gavin?" Eisen said.

"Who's Gavin," Ellen said.

"My information is that Gavin had Ellen followed."

"Jesus Christ," Eisen said. "Will you stop it. Why the fuck would Gavin hire somebody to follow my wife?"

"Darling," Ellen said more firmly, "who is Gavin?"

"He's the chief of security at the shop," Eisen said.

"So why would Gavin have your wife followed?" I said.

"He wouldn't, you idiot, don't you get it?"

"This might go better if you were more restrained," I said.

"Restrained? You're lucky I don't throw you out."

"One of us is," I said.

"What the fuck does that mean?" Eisen said.

I took a deep breath, but it was too late. I found myself standing.

"It means that if you don't settle down I'm going to stick your foot in your ear," I said.

He took an involuntary step backward and realized he had, and tried to compensate.

"You want to try it," he said in a commanding voice.

"Oh, you men," Ellen said. "You're just overgrown boys."

"True," I said. "But it's worth keeping in mind that I'm about thirty pounds more overgrown than your husband."

I looked at Bernie for a moment.

"And, I would guess, four inches taller."

"You think I can't handle myself?" Bernie said.

"You've probably been handling yourself too much," I said.

Ellen giggled. I think we were both startled.

Bernie said, "Ellen, for God's sake."

Ellen said, "Well, it was kind of funny. And, Bernie, get real. Look at him. He's much too big and strong."

"Thank you," I said.

She smiled at me and said, "You're welcome."

"Okay, okay," Bernie said. "We'll let it go for now."

"Whew," I said.

"But I want to know your scam."

"Somebody spiked your open-marriage poster boy three times in the head."

"Open marriage?" Bernie said.

"Darrin and I explained our arrangement to Mr. Spenser," Ellen said.

"I would have thought it was none of his business," Eisen said.

I thought he had a point.

"Oh, aren't you funny?" Ellen said. "Darrin felt it was the right thing to do. You know perfectly well that a relationship cannot be truly open if we are not truly open about it."

Eisen nodded.

"I know, darling. I know."

He looked at me.

"All the more reason that your story doesn't hold water. In a relationship like ours, there's nothing to hide. Why would someone follow either one of us."

"My question exactly," I said.

"Well, my man," Eisen said to me. "If your story is anything but some sort of clumsy attempt to extort money, then I guess you'll have to talk with Steve Gavin. I know nothing about any of this, and I'm sure Ellen doesn't either."

"I don't," Ellen said, "really."

It was quite possible that they didn't. But Bernie knew it had happened. It would have been forcefully explained to him by Gavin, the moment after I left Gavin's office. It had almost certainly also been explained that his mouth should remain firmly shut on the matter. Which it would until I had something to pry it open with. I finished the last of my scotch and soda and put the glass down, centering it on the coaster. Tough guy like Eisen, you couldn't be too careful

"Thanks for your time," I said.

Eisen didn't say anything.

Ellen stood and said, "I'll walk to the door with you."

After she closed the door behind me and while I was waiting for the elevator, I put my ear against the door. But I couldn't hear anything. Maybe there was nothing to hear. Maybe in open marriage you didn't get too attached to your non-spousal partner. Ellen had shown no sign that Trent Rowley's death made any difference to her. I wondered if she'd mourn Bernie. Or Darrin O'Mara. Maybe in open marriage you didn't get too attached to anybody. Easy come, easy go. Maybe open marriage was a crock. In the elevator, going down, I decided that it was.

21

No one was in the office at 9:15 in the morning when I showed up at the Templeton Group. No one arrived. I called them on my cell phone. An answering machine told me that they weren't there to receive my call, but that my call was important to them, and I should leave a message. I left my cell phone number. There was a sort of coffee shop–cafeteria on the lobby floor of 100 Summer, so I went down and ate two donuts and drank some coffee. At 10:30 I called Templeton again. Same machine. Same message. I left my cell phone number.

Back at my office, I opened all the windows so that the fresh exhaust fumes from Berkeley Street could dispel the stale air. Then I got the phone book out and looked up Jerry Francis and Mario Bellini. Neither was in Boston. I called information.

That took a while, but eventually I found Jerry Francis in Dedham and Mario Bellini in Revere. I called them. I got two more answering machines. I left my cell phone number.

I was beginning to feel lonely. I called Elmer O'Neill's number in Arlington. I got a machine. I left my cell phone number. After I hung up I stood for a while looking out my window. The weather was good. There were a number of well-dressed women moving past on Berkeley Street. I honed my surveillance skills on them for a while, and then, in the absence of a better plan, I closed up the office and drove out to Arlington to see if Elmer might show up.

The recycled gas station was closed, and locked. There was no *back in an hour* sign in the window. I sat in my car and did some more work on 411, looking for a home number and address. It was easy. He lived in Arlington, in his office. I got out and went and looked through the office front window. He wasn't in there. On the left wall there was a door to what had probably once been a service bay. I walked around and looked in a small window. It was Elmer's room. He wasn't in it. I drove up to Revere and located Mario Bellini's place on the first floor of a faded three-decker. He wasn't in it. Then I drove down to Dedham and tried Francis's pad in something brick that they probably called a garden apartment. Francis wasn't there. No one answered the door anywhere. Apparently all three lived alone. I called them all a couple more times on the drive back from Dedham. I didn't get anyone. I didn't bother to leave my cell phone number.

In the detective business when every avenue seems closed, the best thing to do is to find a really good-looking woman and solicit her for sex. Susan was still with a patient when I got there, so I went upstairs to her apartment and sat on the couch with Pearl and drank some beer. Susan was as likely to drink beer as she was to bake a cherry pie. But she always kept a few bottles of Blue Moon Belgian White Ale on my account. Which I took to be strong evidence of her love.

In Susan's honor I drank the beer from the English pub glasses that she had bought for that purpose, and I was on the third beer when she came in.

"Last of the whack jobs?" I said.

"I try to think of them as patients," Susan said. "But, yes, I have no more customers today."

She came over and kissed me and Pearl, in that order, which I took to be another strong sign. Then she got herself a glass of white wine and sat on the couch with me, on the side away from Pearl.

"How goes the war on crime?" Susan said.

"Not well," I said. "I can't seem to find any of my witnesses."

"Really?" Susan said. "Would you like to tell me about it?"

"Of course," I said. "Why did you think I came here?"

"Sex," Susan said.

"Besides that," I said.

"Tell me about it," she said.

I did.

"Do you think anything has happened to them?" Susan said.

"There could be a hundred reasons why none of them is at their post," I said.

"But it is somewhat coincidental that all three of them are not at their post simultaneously."

"Yes," I said. "It is."

I got careless with my beer glass for a moment, and Pearl

slurped in a fast tongueful before I moved it to a more secure location.

"It's only dog slobber," Susan said.

"Nothing wrong with dog slobber," I said.

"Of course there isn't," Susan said. "What are you going to do now?"

"Finish the beer," I said.

"No." Susan smiled. "I meant about the missing people?"

"I'll keep trying," I said. "Probably talk with Gavin again."

"Think you'll get anything from Gavin?"

"Probably not."

"What do you want to know?" Susan said.

"Ultimately I want to know who killed Trent Rowley. But in order to do that it might help if I knew why Gavin was having people followed."

Susan said, "Perhaps Darrin O'Mara would be worth a talk."

"Matters of the Heart?"

"Un-huh. You mentioned that Ellen considers him her advisor."

"And she might have sought his advice," I said, "on other matters?"

"I believe that Darrin," Susan said, "would argue that all matters are of the heart."

"He would," I said.

Susan turned her palms up in a gesture that said, "Well?"

She sipped her wine. I finished my beer. Pearl watched us intently.

"Do you think matters of the heart includes matters of the libido?" I said.

"Of course it does," she said. "The distinction is artificial."

"So love and desire are aspects of the same thing?"

"Um hm."

"And you love me," I said.

"Oh, oh!" Susan said.

I looked at her and waited.

"What about the baby?" Susan said.

"We could let her watch."

"Oh, ick!"

"Or not," I said.

"I do have a soup bone in the refrigerator," Susan said, "that I keep for emergencies such as this."

"So could we leave her here on the couch?" I said. "With the bone, sneak into your bedroom, and reconsider the connection between libido and love? While, oblivious, she gnaws happily away out here?"

"We'd be fools not to," Susan said.

22

Gavin was waiting for me with two other guys in the hallway outside my office when I came to work in the morning carrying a large coffee in a paper cup.

"Spenser," he said, "we need to talk."

"Sure we do," I said.

Gavin looked as chrome-plated and slick as he had the last time. The two men with him wore dark blazers and light gray slacks. On the breast pocket of each blazer the name Kinergy was spelled out in jagged script so it resembled a lightning bolt. Beneath the logo was the word *Security.* I unlocked the door and we went in. They came in after me and the last one closed the door. Gavin went to the client chair with arms. The other two men sat on the couch. It was Pearl's couch, but she wasn't with me, so I made no objection.

"Now," Gavin said. "We need to talk."

"You mentioned that," I said.

Carefully, I took the plastic lid off my coffee and tossed it in the wastebasket.

"We'd like to hire you," Gavin said.

"You three?" I said.

Gavin was not amused.

"No, no," he said. "Kinergy."

"So what are these guys for, to carry the money?"

"Our pipeline division is encountering vandalism problems, and we would like to employ you to look into that."

"Wow," I said. "Where are the problems taking place?"

"You'd be working out of our Tulsa office," Gavin said.

"Tulsa," I said.

"The pay would be ample and you'd be on full-time expenses. Everything first class. We have a very generous expense account policy."

"Tulsa," I said. "To track down vandals."

"And," Gavin said, "when you finish in Tulsa, there'd be other work. Southern California, for instance, or Vancouver."

"You got any problems in Paris?" I said.

"We have an office in Paris," Gavin said.

"Sacre bleu," I said.

"What?"

"Excuse me," I said. "I speak so many languages . . ." Gavin obviously didn't know what I was talking about.

"So," he said. "You have an interest? You could pretty well name your price."

"How about the Templeton Group, or Elmer O'Neill?" I said. "What price did they name?"

"Excuse me?"

"I just wondered about your other hires," I said.

"I'm sorry, we haven't hired anybody."

"I was misinformed," I said.

"So," Gavin said brightly, "you interested?"

"Nope."

Gavin was silent for a moment, his eyes behind the thick glasses getting narrow.

Then he said, "Think about this, Spenser. This is a good deal for you. This is a chance to establish a long-term relationship with what may be the greatest company in the country."

"You wouldn't know who killed Trent Rowley, would you?" I said.

"That is a police matter," Gavin said. "We are permitting the police to handle it."

"So you haven't offered them a trip to Tulsa," I said.

Gavin's eyes were now so narrow it was surprising that he could still see.

"I am trying to conduct this meeting in a businesslike and professional manner," he said. "You do not make that easy."

"Thanks for noticing," I said.

Gavin was silent for a considerable time, giving me the slit-eyed stare, tapping his fingertips gently together under his chin. While he did that I used the time to look at the other two guys. They looked like they'd been hired for their looks, sent over by a casting company to play high-powered corporate security guys. One had a dark crew cut. The other had shaved his head. They were about six feet tall, the shaved-head guy a little taller, and they looked as if they got a lot of exercise.

When he'd softened me up enough with the flinty stare, Gavin finally spoke. His voice was flat, and measured like a guy trying to overcome a stutter.

"We pride ourselves," he said, "on being a can-do company. If the conventional businesslike and professional approaches are closed to us, we find other ways."

I nodded enthusiastically.

"I admire that in any organization," I said and looked at the guys on the couch, "don't you?"

Neither of them answered. Gavin spoke again.

"Do you understand what I am saying to you?"

"Same thing you've been saying since you came in with the Righteous Brothers. You don't want me trying to find out what happened to Trent Rowley. Or why you put a tail on Ellen Eisen and Marlene Rowley."

Gavin hardened his stare, which was no easy task.

"I don't know what you're talking about," Gavin said slowly. "I came here to offer you a chance to make some serious money. You not only declined, you did so in an offensive manner, and I am just reminding you that we at Kinergy are used to getting what we want."

"You know what would be really helpful to me?" I said.

"What?"

"If you could teach me that stare. I could frighten the knob off a door if I had that stare."

Gavin held the stare for a moment, but he couldn't keep it up and shifted his gaze to the window behind me.

From the couch the shaved-head guy said, "Mr. Gavin, if it was okay with you, maybe we could teach him some manners."

"Eeek," I said.

Gavin kept looking out my window for a couple of beats. I suspected he was counting. Then he shifted his gaze back to me.

"Not this time, Larry," he said. "Not this time."

"Larry?" I said. "How can you have an enforcer named Larry?"

Larry said, "You think there's something funny about my name, pal?"

"With your name," I said. "With your act. With your haircut."

"Larry," Gavin said. "Shut up."

Gavin stood. The two men on the couch stood.

"I want you to think hard on this," Gavin said to me, bending slightly forward. "And we'll come back soon and make you the offer again."

"Oh good," I said. "It'll give purpose to my week."

Nobody seemed to have anything to say about that, so, after a moment, the three of them turned and marched out.

23

I was in my office, thinking, when Marlene Rowley came in. Today she was wearing big sunglasses and a low-cut red linen dress. I was relieved to see her. Thinking is hard.

"I'm on my way to the Gainsborough exhibit," she said, "and I thought I'd stop by and get a report."

"Would you settle for a few questions?"

"I did not employ you to ask questions," she said.

"Didn't we already go through this?" I said.

She sat down across the desk from me and crossed her legs, sort of immodestly, I thought. Maybe we were getting more intimate. Last time it had been only kneecaps.

"So, may I assume that you have no new information on my husband's death?"

"I have information all over me," I said. "But I don't know what to do with it."

"Do you know who killed Trent?"

"Not yet."

"Have you enough information to exonerate me from any possible complicity?"

"No."

"Well, for God's sake," she said. "What have you been doing?"

"Suffering fools gladly," I said.

"Well . . . may I assume that I am exempt from that remark?"

"Sure," I said. "Did you know that you were being followed?"

"Followed?"

"Yep. Guy named Jerry Francis, from a small agency named the Templeton Group."

"Detective agency?"

"Yep."

"I was being followed by a private detective."

"You were."

"How could you possibly know that?"

"I caught him," I said. "I had reason to think someone was following you and I went out and waited for him to show up and when he did, we talked."

"You did that for me?" she said.

I smiled winningly.

"Part of the service," I said.

"You watched over me."

"We never sleep," I said.

She would have been making me uncomfortable if I weren't so sophisticated.

"My God, that's so sweet," she said.

"You have thoughts on who might hire a detective to fol-low you?"

She stood suddenly and walked around my desk and bent over and put her arms around my neck. I realized she was going to kiss me and moved my face enough so she got me on the right cheek. She stood back.

"Most men kiss me back," she said. "On the mouth."

"I don't blame them," I said.

"Why didn't you?"

"Regretfully," I said, "I'm in love with another woman."

"That Susan what's her name," she said.

"Silverman," I said.

"I didn't know she was Jewish."

"No reason you should," I said.

"And that means to you that you may respond to no other woman?"

"It means I shouldn't act on the response," I said.

"Are you and she married?"

"Not exactly," I said.

"And yet you cling to this modern superstition?"

"About monogamy?"

"Yes."

"We do," I said.

"Only in circumstances where love is unbidden," Marlene said, "by law or convention, can it truly be given and received."

"I've heard that," I said.

"It's a truth that goes back to the ancient poets of Provence," she said.

"So the best way to be in love with her is to have sex with somebody else?"

"To be free to love someone else," she said. "Only if you can choose others, can your choice of her be uncoerced."

"By God you're right," I said. "Enough with the love talk, off with the clothes."

"Here?" she said.

She glanced around the office.

"On that couch?" she said.

"Actually I was just trying to lighten the moment with a bit of roguish wit," I said.

She began to cry.

"You are making fun," she said.

"Only a little," I said.

She sat suddenly on the couch and put her hands in her face, sort of dramatically, I thought.

"No one understands me. I can't count on anybody," she said. "I have so much to give, so much love."

I couldn't think of anything to say.

"But I'm strong," she said after a couple of sobs. "I don't need anyone."

She was quiet for a time while she got her crying under control. I offered her a Kleenex from my bottom desk drawer. She took it and dabbed at her eyes. She looked straight at me.

"I'm sorry, but being a widow is very difficult."

"You okay now?"

"In a manner of speaking," she said sadly.

"You have any thoughts on who might have had you followed?" I said.

She stood and stared at me, horrified.

"You go right back to questioning me, you bastard," she said. "You heartless bastard."

She turned and left. I went to my window and stood looking out at Berkeley Street, thinking about courtly love, and the Provençal poets. In a minute she appeared on the sidewalk, and turned right to Boylston, walking purposefully, and right again, onto Boylston and out of sight.

24

The message on my answering machine was from a woman with a prestigious British accent. She said her name was Delia, that she was calling from Kinergy on behalf of Bob Cooper, and that Bob would very much like to meet me for lunch at his club.

The CEO. Hot dog!

Cooper's club was on the top floor of a tall odd-looking building on Franklin Street. I had to sign in and get a pass before I could go in the elevator. Then I had to show my pass and give my name to the reception desk in the sky lobby, before I could take a second elevator to the Standish Club. A dignified woman in a dark suit met me at the elevator.

"Mr. Cooper hasn't arrived yet," she said. "His secretary called to say that he'd be a few minutes late."

Of course he'd be a few minutes late.

"Do you wish to be seated?" the woman said. "Or do you prefer to wait at the bar?"

Only a loser was caught sitting alone at a table waiting for someone.

"Seated," I said.

It did me no harm to be thought a loser. Might even do me some good. She took me to a table by the window, took my order for beer, and left me to admire the water views. Boston being what it was there weren't many high floors downtown where you couldn't see the water. But the Standish Club had made the most of it. There were two floor-to-ceiling window walls facing the water, and the light poured through them and the room gleamed. Near the center of the room was a circular bar with four people trying not to look like losers as they sipped cocktails and waited. They were all men. They all wore business suits. They all wore white shirts. Two had blue ties, one had a red tie. One had yellow. Three had short, but not too short, recent, but not too recent haircuts. The other guy had shoulder-length black hair. He was also the one with the yellow tie. Probably worked in advertising.

I was two swallows into my first beer when Cooper showed up. He walked into the dining room like he was taking a curtain call. He was a big man with a square jaw and bright blue eyes. He wore a light gray summer-weight suit, with a white shirt and a powder blue satin tie. His hair was iron gray and brushed back carefully over the ears. I stood when he reached the table.

"Spenser?" he said. "Bob Cooper, thanks for coming."

"My pleasure," I said.

"Hope you weren't waiting long."

I looked at my watch.

"Ten minutes," I said.

"Hell, I'm sorry. They don't give me a damned minute over there."

"I'm sure they don't," I said.

Without being asked, the waitress brought a tall glass of something bubbly, with an orange slice in it, and placed it in front of Cooper.

Without looking up he said, "Thanks, Shirley."

He picked up the glass, made a toasting gesture at me, and took a sip.

"Campari and soda," he said. "You ever try it?"

"I have," I said.

"Like it?"

"No."

Cooper laughed as if what I'd said was funny. Maybe for him hearing the word *no*, in any context, *was* the sudden perception of incongruity.

"Acquired taste," he said. "You hungry?"

I said I was. He agreed. We both studied the menu for a moment. Then he ordered a Caesar salad. I had a club sandwich.

"So," I said, "Mr. Cooper . . ."

"Coop," he said. "Everybody calls me Coop."

I nodded.

"So what brings us together, Coop?"

"Well, I know you're looking into the death of Trent Rowley, poor bastard, he was a good man, and I thought well, hell, might make sense to talk face-to-face, you know? One working stiff to another, see if we can get somewhere."

"One working stiff to another, Coop?"

He grinned.

"Yeah, yeah. There's probably more bullshit and folderol around my job, but we're both trying to make an honest living."

"Just a couple a working stiffs," I said.

He grinned again. It was a really good grin.

"You actually think somebody in the shop killed Trent?"

"I don't know who killed Trent," I said. "But it had to be somebody that could come and go in the shop without any problem."

The waitress came back with our food. My sandwich had a small heap of French fries with it. I ate one. Shame to waste them.

"Damn," Cooper said. "You got that right, don't you. There's no way in hell to get around it."

My club sandwich was cut in triangular quarters. I took a small dignified bite from one of them. It seemed bad strategy to get it all over my shirtfront.

" 'Course most of the wives know their way around there," he said.

"You think somebody's wife shot Rowley?"

"Hell, I don't know. That's your department. I'm just thinking out loud."

"Any other candidates?" I said. "Besides employees and wives?"

"Oh, hell yes," Cooper said.

He ate very rapidly.

"We got vendors, coming and going. We got customers. Government people, you know, Interior, Commerce, SEC, Energy, State Department."

"State?" I said.

"Yes, we are a very large presence on the international energy scene, we do a lot of business with foreign governments."

"Gee," I said.

"Spenser," he said, "I gotta tell you, we are one hell of a company. We really are."

He was almost finished with his salad. I had three-quarters still to go on my club sandwich. I was betting Coop wasn't the kind of guy that was going to sit around while I finished. He took his last bite of salad. He looked at his watch.

"Goddamn," he said. "I'm already running late on the afternoon."

I knew I should have bet myself money.

"I wanted to get a look at you," he said. "And I'm glad I did. I like what I see."

I smiled modestly.

"Tell you what," Cooper said. "We're having a corporate retreat this weekend, down on the Cape, Chatham Bars Inn. We got the whole place. Informal. Give us all a chance to kick back and get to know each other in a relaxed way, you know, out of the office, away from the phone. We tear up the place pretty good."

I nodded and picked up the second quarter of my club sandwich.

"I was hoping you might join us, as my guest, of course. Get to know all the management people, might help you learn a little about us, and even if it doesn't . . ."

Cooper grinned and winked at me.

"Hell, it's a good time. You married?"

"Sort of," I said.

"Well, bring your sort-of wife along too."

"Actually," I said, "I don't *bring* her anywhere. But she might like to come."

"I'll have Delia send you the details," Cooper said. "She'll reserve a room for you."

"Sure," I said.

He looked at his watch again.

"Gee, look," he said. "I'm sorry. I just have to run."

"Un-huh," I said.

"I hope you don't mind."

"I'm a working stiff myself," I said. "I know how it is."

There was just a flicker on Cooper's face for a moment. Was I kidding him? No, of course not. Bob Cooper? No, couldn't be.

"Well, I look forward to seeing you in Chatham," he said and put out his hand. "I'll buy you a drink."

He grinned again and winked again.

"Maybe several," he said.

25

Darrin O'Mara broadcast from a studio on the seventh floor of an ugly little building near the Fleet Center. I met him when he got off the air, and we went around the corner to a big faux Irish pub for a drink. The Celtics and the Bruins were through for the year, so the place was nearly empty and we were able to sit by ourselves at one end of the bar. O'Mara ordered a pint of Guinness. I didn't want to seem inauthentic, but I couldn't stand Guinness. I ordered a Budweiser.

O'Mara took a sip, and looked pleased. He turned a little toward me, with one elbow on the bar, and said in his soft rich radio voice, "How can I help you?"

"Tell me about Marlene Rowley," I said.

"Marlene Rowley?"

"Yep."

"Why would you think I would have anything to tell you about her?"

"We were talking about, ah, relationships," I said, "and she began to sound like Chrétien de Troyes."

"Really," O'Mara said.

"She was expounding the same flapdoodle about courtly love that Ellen Eisen espouses," I said. "I assumed she got it from the same place."

"I don't believe that the principles of courtly love are flapdoodle," O'Mara said. "Sometimes clients misstate or misunderstand those tenets. But that does not invalidate them."

The bartender was a firm-looking redhead in tight black pants. She was slicing lemons at the other end of the bar. There was a gray-haired couple drinking rye and ginger and chain-smoking in a booth near the door. They didn't talk, or even look at each other.

"Do you know Marlene Rowley?" I said.

"I do, professionally."

"And her husband?"

"Yes," O'Mara said. "They were both in my seminar."

"And the Eisens?" I said. "Same seminar?"

"Yes."

"And, of course the Rowleys knew the Eisens."

"Of course, the husbands were colleagues at Kinergy."

"What kind of seminar is it that they were in?" I said.

"Love and Liberation, it's called."

"Yippee," I said. "Did you know that Ellen Eisen and Trent Rowley were having an affair?"

"They had developed a relationship. It is part of the seminar. Marlene and Bernie were developing a relationship as well."

"A sexual relationship?"

"Of course."

I nodded. I squeezed my eyes shut trying to concentrate.

"So," I said slowly, "were they, in the language of courtly love, wife swapping?"

"They were developing cross-connubial relationships," O'Mara said.

"I'll bet they were," I said.

"My presence here is voluntary, Spenser. I don't have any obligation to sit here and listen to your misinformed disapproval."

I looked at the gray-haired couple in the booth. They each had a fresh rye and ginger. He was staring out the front window of the pub. She was looking at the bottles stacked up behind the bar. Both were smoking. They didn't seem close. Probably rebelling against coercive love.

"Did all four members of this tag team know of the situation?" I said.

"Of course. Everything took place within seminar guidelines."

"So why did Marlene hire me to follow her husband?"

"I have only your word," O'Mara said, "that she did."

"Take as a premise that she did," I said. "Speculate with me."

O'Mara signaled the bartender for another Guinness.

"And a pony of Jameson's," he said. "Beside it."

The bartender looked at me. I nodded yes to another Bud.

"Were that the case," O'Mara said, "perhaps it would indicate that Marlene had failed to transcend the material plane."

"Meaning that if Trent became enamored enough of Ellen to stroll off into the sunset," I said, "Marlene wanted to be sure she'd get hers."

O'Mara was watching the bartender pour the whisky. He seemed relieved when she started back down the bar with it.

"Hypothetically," O'Mara said.

"Any sign that was happening?" I said.

"I am not a dating service," O'Mara said. "I instruct people in a certain philosophy, and I help them understand its implications."

"Do you know anyone named Gavin?" I said.

"Not that I can think of," O'Mara said.

He took a sip of the whisky and washed it with Guinness. He looked happier.

"Bob Cooper?" I said.

"No, I don't believe I know him either," he said.

"And you don't know any reason somebody might shoot Trent Rowley?"

"God no," he said.

"Eisen didn't mind his wife and Trent."

"Absolutely not. Any more than Trent minded Bernie and Marlene."

"And why would anyone," I said.

"Why indeed," O'Mara said.

The Irish boilermaker was cheering him greatly.

"You ever read Chaucer's *Troilus and Criseyde*?" I said.

"If I did," O'Mara said with a smile, "I've forgotten it. Why do you ask?"

"Character named Pandarus," I said. "I was going to ask you about him."

O'Mara polished off the rest of the Irish whisky and gestured at the bartender for another one.

"I fear that you may be misled," he said. "The references to courtly love are metaphoric, if you see what I mean."

The whisky arrived. He took a fond sip and let it trickle down his throat. Then he drank some Guinness.

"My field is not literature," he said. "Though literature is surely a stimulus to my thinking."

He had swung fully around on his barstool, facing the big nearly empty room, with both elbows resting behind him on the bar. I felt a lecture lurking.

"My field," he said, "is human interaction."

"You and Linda Lovelace," I said.

I left O'Mara at the bar. As I came out, I saw a guy with shoulder-length black hair round the corner onto Causeway Street and disappear.

I only saw his back, but the hair looked like the guy I'd seen at Bob Cooper's club.

26

Healy came into my office with a bag of donuts and two large cups of coffee. He sat and handed me a coffee.

"Dunkin' Donuts," he said. "I get the cop discount."

He held the bag of donuts toward me and I took one. Cinnamon, my favorite.

"I thought it might be time for us to compare notes," Healy said.

"Wow," I said. "You are really stuck, huh?"

"Here's what we know," Healy said. "Somebody shot Trent Rowley to death."

I waited. Healy didn't say anything.

After a while I said, "That much."

"Just barely," Healy said. "Whaddya got?"

"What have I got, just like that? A cup of coffee and a donut and I spill my guts to you?"

"That was my plan," Healy said.

We each drank some coffee. Healy and I had been sort of friends for a long time. Which did not mean I needed to tell him everything I knew unless there was something in it for me. There might be.

"The security guy at Kinergy," I said. "Gavin. He hired two, ah, marginal private eyes to follow the wives of a couple of his employees, including Marlene Rowley."

"Tell me about that," Healy said.

I told him.

"And you can't find either gumshoe," Healy said.

"Maybe I just keep missing them," I said.

"Maybe. I'll have someone run it down."

"Can you let me know?" I said.

"As quick as you did," Healy said.

I gave him my big charming smile.

"Better late than never," I said.

"Yeah," Healy said, "sure."

My big charming smile generally worked better with women.

"What's Gavin have to say about it?"

"Denies everything."

"And he paid them cash."

"Yep."

"So the only way we know he hired them to do the tail job is because they told you."

"Yep."

"And now you can't find them."

"So far," I said.

"So unless we find them we have no evidence that Gavin did anything except what you say they told you."

"Exactly," I said.

"We know how much that's worth," Healy said.

"Sadly, yes," I said.

"Hell, even if it was worth anything it doesn't prove it was Gavin; there's a lot of blond guys with mustaches."

"I know," I said. "It would have to be an ID by O'Neill or Francis."

"Which we can't get if we can't find them."

Healy and I both took a bite of donut and looked at each other while we chewed.

When he was through chewing, Healy swallowed and said, "Might be we won't find them."

"That occurred to me," I said.

"Still, we got Gavin," Healy said.

"For what?"

"For looking into," Healy said.

"It's a start," I said.

27

Susan was wearing white pants that fit well, and a top with horizontal blue and white stripes and a wide scoopy neck which revealed the fact that she had the best-looking trapezius muscles of any woman in the world. I was nearly as dashing, though flaunting it less, in jeans and sneakers and a black tee shirt. I was carrying a gun so I wore the tee shirt not tucked in. We were sitting in the lobby at the Chatham Bars Inn amid a maelstrom of yuppies, mostly male, in bright Lacoste shirts, maroon and green predominating, pressed khakis, and moccasins, mostly cognac-colored, no socks. The women followed the same color scheme, the khaki varying among slacks, skirts, and shorts, depending, Susan and I agreed, on how they felt about their legs. Bob Cooper moved among them, wearing a starched white button-down shirt, top two buttons open, black linen trousers, and black Italian loafers: the patriarch, his gray head visible among the acolytes, laughing, squeezing shoulders, hugging an occasional woman, accepting obeisance. Gavin moved always near Cooper, wearing one of those white-nipped long-waisted shirts that Cubans wear in Miami. Bernie Eisen was there, drinking mai tais. I saw no sign of Ellen.

The chatter was continuous and loud. It was the first day of the retreat, cocktail time, and everyone was taking full advantage. The company had rented the whole place. Everyone there was from Kinergy, except me and Susan.

"Breathtaking," Susan said, "isn't it."

"Think of the pressure," I said. "Do I look like a winner? Am I dressed right? Am I talking to the right people? Have I signed up for the right activities? What if I've signed up for sailing and it turns out that only losers sign up for sailing?"

"You can smell the fear," Susan said. "And the greed."

"That too," I said.

"We have penetrated to the heart," Susan said, "of corporate America."

"Have you noticed that Cooper is the tallest guy in the room?" I said.

"He is a tall man."

"He's not much taller than I am."

"So you would be the second tallest?" Susan said.

"You think it is an accident that no member of Kinergy management is as tall as the CEO?" I said.

Susan was holding a glass of pinot grigio, from which she had, in theory, been drinking for an hour and ten minutes. It was down nearly half an inch. She took another sip, and swallowed, looking at the room. Her lips were slightly parted, the residue of wine making them gleam. I knew that jumping over there and sitting on her lap was unseemly. I fought the impulse back.

"We only assume something to be an accident when all other explanations fail," she said.

"Wow," I said. "Is that the royal we? Or are you talking about you and me?"

"You and me," she said. "I only use the royal we for state occasions."

"So you think it's an accident?"

"No."

"Couldn't you have said that to start?"

"I have a Ph.D.," Susan said. "From Harvard. If I had done postdoctoral work I wouldn't be able to speak at all."

"Of course," I said.

"Everyone appears to work out," Susan said.

"And spend a lot of time in the sun," I said.

"There are other ways to appear tanned," Susan said.

"And everyone has even white teeth."

"There are several ways to achieve that also."

"My God," I said. "Is nothing as it appears."

"You and me, Cookie."

"Besides that," I said.

"I think Hawk looks pretty much like who he is."

"I'll tell him," I said. "He'll be proud."

"What do you suppose he and Pearl are doing?"

"Right now?"

"Yes."

"Running along the river, scaring people."

"How nice for her," Susan said.

Set up around the lobby were display posters listing the various events. Every event was a competition in which points could be earned: sailing, fishing, tennis, golf, bocce, badminton, horseshoes, skeet, archery, and a three-mile run. There were shopping trips arranged for the few wives in attendance.

"You think bringing your wife is the mark of a loser?" I said to Susan.

"Absolutely," Susan said. "It certifies that you're pussy whipped."

"I brought you."

"I rest my case," Susan said.

Bob Cooper appeared before us with a drink in his big strong-looking hands. Gavin was with him.

"Spenser," he said, "it's great you could come."

"It is," I said.

"This the sort-of wife?" he said.

"Bob Cooper," I said. "Susan Silverman."

He bowed and shook her hand, smiling at her full wattage.

"If you were sort of my wife, I'd make sure it was the complete deal," he said.

"Actually *sort of* is as far as I want to go," Susan said.

Cooper straightened and put his head back and laughed. It was a big laugh, full of authority.

"Well hell," he said. "Just like a man. I never thought of that."

He glanced at Gavin.

"Gav, you know Spenser, this is, ah, Ms. Silverman."

We shook hands with Gavin just as if we were glad to see him.

"Room suitable?" he said.

"Lovely," Susan said.

Cooper nodded like it actually mattered to him.

"You need anything you call Delia, she's here. Room eleven."

I nodded. Susan smiled.

"I've saved a couple of seats at my table," Cooper said. "For dinner. I hope you can join me."

"We'd be thrilled," Susan said, just as if she meant it.

"See you then," Cooper said. "Dinner's at seven."

He moved off toward a group of men at the bar. Gavin followed. Susan watched them go, smiling.

"Why exactly was it we decided to come to this?"

"I don't know what else to do," I said. "I'm rummaging."

Susan nodded. Her eyes had a little glitter in them. Something was amusing her.

"What?" I said.

"You could barely force yourself to be civil," Susan said. "How long do you suppose that you would last as a Kinergy employee?"

"I suppose it would depend on how much I needed the job," I said.

Susan looked straight at me and gave me a full-out, unfettered grin. My alimentary canal tightened. I took in some air. When she did the unfettered grin, I always felt as if I needed more oxygen than I was getting.

"No," she said. "It wouldn't."

28

Susan and I had dinner with Bob Cooper, at a table that also included Gavin, Bernie Eisen, and a flamboyantly good-looking dark-haired woman named Adele McCallister, whose title was elaborate and failed to reveal what she did. Cooper was at his smart, good-old-boy best, charming to all, and especially charming with Susan. Gavin was genially cryptic, and Bernie Eisen did his very best impression of a masculine winner.

Adele flirted with me through Susan.

"Well," she said, "Susan, he's a big one, isn't he?"

Susan smiled at her. It was like old money and nouveau riche. Susan was good-looking, as if her family had been good-looking for seven generations. It was as much a part of her as her intelligence.

"Would you like to feel his muscles?" Susan said.

"Is he really as muscular as he looks?" Adele said.

"Fearful," Susan said.

"Is that right?" Adele said, looking at me.

"Fearful," I said.

"May I feel?"

"I can't make a muscle," I said. "It will tear my coat."

"Somebody said you used to be a fighter," Bob said.

"Who?" I said.

"Oh, I can't recall, but there's some scarring around your eyes."

"You used to box?" Adele said.

"Not everyone thought so," I said.

"Oh, isn't that cute," Adele said to Susan. "He's being modest."

Susan's eyes gleamed at me for a moment.

"He has much to be modest about," Susan said.

"Let me ask you this," Adele said. "If all you men had a fight, would you win?"

Adele's question had a nasty little undertone.

"Question's really aimless," I said. "Anybody can beat anybody. It's only a matter of who wants it more."

"Boxing is not the only martial art," Gavin said.

"Absolutely," Bernie said. "Absolutely."

Cooper watched it all as if he weren't a part of it, an observer, open-shuttered and passive. He seemed especially interested in Bernie. Adele slid her hand over and squeezed my upper arm. I was too vain not to flex.

"Oh my God," she said, and looked at Susan. "Does he hurt?"

"Only in the cutest way," Susan said.

Bob Cooper paid us every heed. Bernie Eisen told some jokes. Gavin maintained his reserve. Susan and I fought Adele off for the rest of the meal. After dinner while the Kinergy winners crowded into the bar for Irish cream on the rocks, Susan and I went up to our room.

In the elevator I said to Susan, "When we go into our room, don't say anything until I tell you."

"Why, do you think there's some sort of device?"

"How did he know I boxed?" I said.

"Healy must have talked to him," Susan said. "Maybe Healy told him."

"Healy doesn't tell anybody anything," I said.

"No, you're right. His business is to know, not to tell."

"Like you."

Susan smiled.

"My business is to keep Adele from climbing in through your fly," Susan said.

"Ever vigilant," I said.

"So CEO Bob must have been checking on you."

"And he might want to know more," I said.

The elevator door opened and we went to our room.

29

Susan sat near the window and looked out and was quiet while I looked for a bug. It was in the bowl of a ceiling lamp. Whoever put it in wasn't very inventive. It was the first place I looked. I took it out and put it in my pocket. Sometimes, if the subject probably expects to be bugged, you put in one he'll find easily and another one much harder to find, hoping that he'll think that disabling the first one takes care of it. I didn't think they expected me to look for a bug, but I snooped around the rest of the place anyway. No second bug. I took the one I'd found and flushed it down the toilet.

"That should make an interesting transmission," Susan said. "Are we free to talk?"

"Let's risk it," I said.

"Why would they bug our room?"

"To confirm my reputation as a sexual Goliath."

"Lucky you found the bug," Susan said. "Another reason?"

"Same reason Coop's been schmoozing me, same reason they invited me. They want to get a handle on me, they want to know what I know."

"So you feel that they're involved in Rowley's death?"

"Don't know. They could just be trying to make it go away so they can return to the unfettered pursuit of profit."

"Do you really think," Susan said, "that one murder would have a serious effect on their business."

I didn't say anything. Susan waited.

"Well," she said. "Do you?"

"No," I said.

"So, there's something more," she said.

"So, there is," I said.

"I think Coop's plan includes charming you," Susan said, "so you'll think he's swell, and Kinergy is swell, and nobody there could ever do something bad."

"That would be a lot of charm."

"Does Coop think he has lots of charm?"

"Of course," I said. "Never is heard a discouraging word."

"Of course it's really because he has power," Susan said.

"But he probably doesn't know the difference," I said.

"Or chooses not to."

We were standing together looking out the window at the ocean-washed sand shoals that gave Chatham Bars Inn its name. There were some people on the beach, and some boats on the water, and blue distance beyond. I had my arm around Susan's shoulder. She had her arm around my waist.

"That was sort of ugly," Susan said, "Adele's question about if there was a fight would you win."

"I know. She must resent all the testosterone."

"It put the men in an impossible position unless one of them wanted to challenge you."

"Which would have been unseemly."

"And quite possibly dangerous," Susan said. "You are not exactly the Easter Bunny."

"Gavin tried a little," I said.

"Yes. The remark about martial arts. Do you think he's dangerous?"

"Sure."

"Do you think you could beat him up?"

"Sure."

"If you could keep her from molesting you," Susan said, "Adele might be interesting to talk with."

"If she knows anything."

"She must know something worth hearing. And she doesn't like those men."

"And might take pleasure in ratting them out?" I said.

"Discreetly," Susan said. "By innuendo. In the guise of being feminine, or witty, or simply *so* cute and sexy."

Susan put her head against my shoulder while we looked at the ocean.

"I don't want to sound sexually incorrect," I said, "but do you think she slept her way up the corporate ladder?"

"Adele?" Susan said. "Does a cat have an ass?"

"Okay," I said. "It's a job that's got to be done."

"And don't you dare enjoy it," Susan said.

It was getting dark. The beach had emptied. The wind was quiet. The water moved more gently. The blue distance had shortened and darkened as it closed down onto the horizon.

"Pretty much," I said. "I think we enjoy each other."

"Yes," Susan said. "A lot."

30

Coop gave it one more try at breakfast. Susan and I were at a table by the window, where I was eating corned beef hash with a poached egg, and Susan was nursing half a bagel. Carrying a cup of coffee, Bob strode across the room trailing a gentle hint of expensive cologne. He pulled over a chair from another table, turned it around and sat straddling it with his forearms resting on the back.

"Hope I'm not interrupting," he said.

"Not at all," I said. "We were just speaking aimlessly of our hopes and dreams."

Coop smiled.

"You are a kidder, aren't you?"

"Makes me fun to be around," I said.

"Sure does," Coop said. "Whadda you think, Susan."

"Fun," she said.

She broke off a corner of her bagel and dabbed on a teardrop-sized smudge of cream cheese. Coop watched her for a moment. Then he looked back at me.

"Well," Coop said to me, "on that very subject, I'd like to make you a little offer."

"You'd like to employ me to look into Rowley's death," I said.

Coop was startled. It was maybe the first actual feeling I'd seen him show.

"Well," he said. "Yes. How did you know?"

"Because I turned down your pipe surveillance offer in Tulsa."

"Tulsa?"

"Yeah. Tulsa in June is always tempting, but I couldn't leave Susan."

Coop looked genuinely confused.

"Who made you that offer?" he said.

I grinned at him.

"Gav," I said.

"Oh, well, I try not to micromanage. Are you interested in my offer?" He grinned. "I'm the CEO, it supersedes Gav's offer."

"Rank has its privileges," I said.

"Damn straight," Coop said. "You interested?"

"No," I said.

"Could I ask why?"

"I have a client," I said.

"And our interests coincide. Wouldn't it be better for Marlene if we assumed the cost of investigating her husband's death? She's a widow. Her resources may not be limitless."

"I don't know if your interests coincide," I said. "The only way I'll know that is by doing my work."

"You might consider working for us both. We could certainly improve upon your fee."

"Same answer," I said.

"He's a stubborn one, Susan."

"But fun to be around," Susan said.

Coop studied me for a moment. The rest of the Kinergy revelers were drifting in for breakfast, most of them lining up for the vast buffet.

"I'm a businessman," Coop said. "And if I can't close a deal one way, I come around at it from a different direction."

I ate some hash.

"How about coming aboard as a consultant?"

I smiled.

"Consultant Spenser," I said.

"We could give you a pretty substantial consulting fee."

"And I would advise Gavin on matters of security."

"As needed," Bob said.

He grinned.

"No heavy lifting," he said. "You'd be free to pursue your own cases as well."

"And Rowley's death?"

"Anything you discovered you could share with us, help us provide maximum assistance to the police."

"That's all?"

"Sure," Coop said.

I looked at Susan.

"That's all," I said to her.

"How nice," she said.

Her bagel was nearly a third gone. She must have been ravenous.

"Coop," I said. "Susan and I will be driving home after breakfast. Let us think about your offer."

"Sure thing," Cooper said. "We'd like to have you aboard, Big Guy."

"Thanks, Coop."

Cooper got up and moved through the room. He stopped at several tables, putting his hand on shoulders, patting backs, laughing, bending over to confide.

"Coop," Susan said.

"He likes me," I said "He really, really likes me."

"What's this about Tulsa?"

"I'll tell you on the ride home," I said.

"What do you think he wants?" Susan said.

"He wants to know what I know."

"So he's fearful you'll discover something unfortunate for him or his company."

"Which means," I said, "that there is something unfortunate to discover."

"And," Susan said, "he knows what it is. Do you suppose he'll try to buy off the cops too?"

"He won't get anywhere with Healy," I said. "But Healy's a state employee. You run a company like Kinergy, you have state access."

"There was a time," Susan said, "when you would have told Coop to go fuck himself."

"True."

"And were he to have objected, you would have offered to hit him."

"Impetuous youth," I said.

"Now you are pleasant, for you, and say you'll think about it."

"Balanced maturity," I said. "I sometimes learn more by being pleasant."

Susan smiled. "And," she said, "you can always offer to hit him later."

"And might," I said.

We finished breakfast and got our luggage. Susan carried my small overnight bag. I carried her big bag, and her smaller one, and the one that contained her makeup, and one she referred to as the big poofy one, and a large straw hat she had worn to the beach, which didn't fit into anything.

"Why don't you get a bellman," Susan said.

"Are you trying to compromise my manhood?" I said.

"Oh, yeah, that," she said. "Now and then I forget."

I loaded the back of the car.

"Make sure to open up my big bag so it lies flat," Susan said.

I did, and closed the trunk lid, and walked around to get in. As I opened the door on my side, I got a glimpse in the outside rearview mirror of a smallish man with long dark hair going into the hotel. I turned for a better look, but he was gone.

"Just one minute," I said to Susan.

I walked back across the parking lot and into the lobby. There was no smallish man with long black hair. I looked in the dining room. Nothing. I glanced at the bar off the lobby, but it was closed until noon. I gave it up and went back out and got in the car.

"Looking for something?" she said.

"Thought I saw someone I knew," I said.

31

Hawk and Pearl were sitting on Susan's front steps when we got back from Chatham. Hawk was drinking a bottle of beer and watching the Radcliffe girls go by. Pearl was sitting beside him with her tongue out. None of us could say for sure what she was looking at. Susan and I accepted, because we were responsible parents, about ten minutes of lapping and cavorting and jumping up as Pearl welcomed us home. Hawk watched silently.

When Pearl finally settled down, Hawk said, "Got a friend owns a dog. She comes home, the dog wags its tail. She pats it on the head, and they both go 'bout their business."

"Your point?" Susan said.

Hawk grinned.

"Jess a wry observation, missy."

"Well, just keep it to yourself," Susan said. "Did the Radcliffe students think my baby was adorable, when they went by?"

"Most of them," Hawk said, "looking at me."

That was probably true. There were few things less Cantabrigian than Hawk. We unloaded Susan's luggage and hauled it to her room.

"Don't seem like you been gone this long," Hawk said.

"Susan packs for all possibilities," I said.

"Like dinner with Louis the Fourteenth."

"Sure," I said. "Cocktails with God. You don't ever know."

"Readiness be all," Hawk said.

"Sho nuff," I said.

Hawk and I drank beer on the front porch while Susan sorted and hung and smoothed and fluffed and folded and caressed and put away the stuff she had packed. Then she got a glass of Riesling and joined us on the front porch.

It wasn't really a porch made to sit on in the evening when it was hot and drink lemonade and listen to the ball game and listen to insects buzz gently outside the screen. It was more of a porch for standing on while you rang the bell. But Susan had put a couple of cute chairs out there, and there was a big railing and five stairs. Susan and I sat in the cute chairs. Hawk draped himself over the railing with his feet up. He always seemed relaxed and he always seemed comfortable.

"Drinking beer on the front porch," I said. "I really should be in my undershirt."

"The wife-beater kind," Susan said, "like a tank top."

"The wife-beater kind?" Hawk said. "Undershirt bigotry?"

"Shocking, isn't it?" Susan said.

"There's a guy I keep seeing around," I said to Hawk. "Small guy, skinny, long black hair, pale skin, little round wire-rimmed glasses."

"Bad guy?"

"Maybe," I said.

"You think he tailing you?"

"Maybe."

"Don't know him," Hawk said.

"Is that who you went back in to look for," Susan said, "at the hotel?"

"Just got a glimpse, might not even be the same guy," I said.

"Way to find out," Hawk said.

"He follows me, you follow him?" I said.

"That be one way. Or he follows you and I follow him and when we establish that he is following you, we take him by the neck and shake him a little and say who dat?"

"Who dat?" I said.

"Who dat," Hawk said, "in dere saying . . ."

Susan said, "Stop it."

Hawk grinned at her.

". . . who dat out dere," he said.

Susan put her fingers in her ears.

"You don't like classic ethnic humor?" Hawk said.

Susan kept her fingers in her ears and shut her eyes tight.

"You Jews are always putting us down," Hawk said.

Susan smiled and opened her eyes.

"We try," Susan said. "God knows we try."

"If I could interrupt for a moment," I said. "When he starts following me again, I'll let you know."

"Usual rate?" Hawk said.

"Absolutely," I said. "In fact I'm thinking about doubling it."

"What is the usual rate?" Susan said.

"Zip," Hawk said.

Susan looked at Hawk and then at me. She drank some Riesling, and shook her head and spoke in a funny voice.

"All the biracial pairs in all the world," she said, "and I end up with you guys."

"That's the best Bogart impression I've ever heard by a woman," I said.

A man wearing a Greek fisherman's hat walked by with a mongrel dog on a leash. Pearl dashed to the fence and barked ferociously. The mongrel growled and pulled on his leash. The man looked annoyed. He glanced up at us sitting on the porch.

"Cute," Hawk said, "isn't she?"

The man stared at Hawk for a moment and then nodded enthusiastically.

"She's very cute," he said and moved his dog briskly along.

Pearl glared after them, still barking, until they turned the corner. Then she padded back up onto the porch and sat and waited to be patted. Susan patted her.

"And how many women have you heard do Bogie?" Susan said.

I thought about it for a moment.

"Zip," I said.

Susan stood. Pearl moved over near Hawk, who patted her.

"I think I'll get us more to drink," Susan said.

We watched her go.

"I love that woman," Hawk said.

"Me too."

32

Adele McCallister's secretary was a sturdy gray-haired woman in a dark dress.

"Ms. McCallister is expecting you," she said and ushered me into the big corner office.

It was all a corner office was supposed to be. Leather couch, entertainment console, a large map of the world marked with colorful tacks. There was a round conference table by the window, and an oriental rug on the floor, a wet bar, and at the back wall of the office, facing the door, and dominating all before it, a long table with elegant legs, which served as a desk. Behind it was Adele, wearing a low-necked pink suit with a short skirt. She had pearls around her neck.

"Pearls go great with the suit," I said.

She smiled.

"I'm working on demure," she said.

I smiled back.

"You might have to work harder," I said.

"Good," she said.

There were original oils on the two inside walls, a couple of which were pretty good.

"Coffee?" she said. "Water? A drink?"

"Coffee."

"Let's have it at the conference table," she said. "Get a better view of the Burger King."

I don't know quite how she knew, but the sturdy secretary appeared almost as soon as we sat, bearing a silver service with a carafe of coffee and cream, sugar, and Equal.

Adele said, "Thank you, Dotty. Hold my calls, please."

Dotty set the tray down, smiled at her boss, and went out. Adele poured us each coffee, into white china mugs, and offered me cream in a silver pitcher. Her mug had "Legs" written on it. It went with the rest of the elegant service like pearls went with a hot pink suit.

"So," Adele said. "Business or pleasure."

"I'm still trying to find out what happened to Trent Rowley," I said. "I was hoping you'd help."

"I'd love to help you," she said.

The way she talked, everything sounded like it would lead to sex.

"Tell me about Trent," I said.

"Trent," she said and leaned back with her elbows resting on the arms of her chair. She drank some of her coffee, holding the cup in both hands. "Trent, Trent, Trent."

I waited.

"You were at Chatham," she said.

"I was."

"With an amazing-looking woman, I might add," Adele said.

"I was."

"You saw what they are, Trent was like the rest of them."

"Which is?"

"Hyperthyroid frat boys out to prove they've got the biggest dick," Adele said.

"By?" I said.

"By bringing in the most business, coming up with the best new scheme, getting the biggest bonus. Kinergy is a money machine if you're good, and willing to work eighteen-hour days, every day."

"Every day?"

"Saturdays, Sundays, and holidays," Adele said. "Some of the losers take Christmas morning off."

"Where do you fit in?" I said.

She grinned and drank some coffee.

"Hyperthyroid sorority girl," she said. "Intent on proving I've got everything the boys have."

"How's that going?" I said.

"I'm doing fine," she said and made an inclusive gesture at the rest of her office.

"What is it you do, exactly?"

"I'm senior vice president for development," she said.

"Yeah?"

"I fly around in the company jet and look for opportunities for us."

"For Kinergy?"

"Sure."

"And that includes what?"

"Mostly blowing the smoke and arranging the mirrors," she said.

"Anything else?" I said. "Anything more, ah, specific."

She smiled widely.

"An occasional BJ," she said.

"An indispensable negotiating tool," I said.

"Nice choice of words."

I shrugged.

"And what did Trent do?"

"CFO," she said.

"Was he good at it?"

"In some ways he was a wizard. He truly understood the manipulation of money. He was a genius at accounting. He understood banking. He had a . . . an almost genetic sense of how Wall Street works."

"That sounds like a wizard in all ways," I said.

"It does," she said. "But . . . it wasn't what he knew and didn't know. It was . . . hell, it was that he didn't want it badly enough."

"Want what?"

"The whole enchilada," Adele said. "Money, power, country club, Porsche, Rolex, Montblanc pen."

"What else is there?" I said.

"It's the way we keep score," Adele said. "And Trent played that game as hard as he could. But there was always . . . I don't know . . . he always seemed to be looking for something that Kinergy doesn't have." She shrugged. "Purpose, peace, love, some philosophical something. I mean Trent could be as big a prick as anyone. And he was a real player . . . but there was that something lacking."

"Or vice versa," I said.

"What? Oh, yes. Maybe not. Maybe it was a good thing. But not here. You want to be here, you can't be good . . . and survive."

"He didn't," I said.

"Yeah. That's kind of sad. But I didn't mean it that way."

"You good?" I said.

"God, no. I'm talking to you because I can't think of any reason not to. But, no, I'd lie to you in a heartbeat. If it would get me something I wanted, I'd sleep with you."

"Be a treat in itself," I said.

She paused and looked at me as if she were considering a purchase.

"Probably would be," she said. "But it would waste a fuck."

"Because I can't do anything for you."

"That's right."

"And you want the whole enchilada?"

"All of it," she said. "Everything the men want, and to get it I have to be better than the men and when I am, I get to rub their noses in it."

"My God," I said. "A feminist."

"Fuck that," she said. "I'm not doing anything for women. I'm doing it for me."

"What can you tell me about Cooper?" I said.

"Wants to be senator, as a way of positioning himself to run for president."

"Hell of a pay cut," I said.

Robert B. Parker

"His focus is upward and out," she said. "Trent and Bernie
Eisen ran the place."

"And now it's just Bernie," I said.

"Yeah. But that'll change. Bernie hasn't got the cojónes or
the smarts without Trent to help him."

"What's Cooper like?"

"God knows," she said. "He might even be what he seems.
I don't know. Mostly he's an absentee landlord. Spends a lot of
time in D.C."

"He married?"

Adele smiled a little.

"Big Wilma," she said.

"Big Wilma."

"She's the wife he married in college and never should have.
But he can't divorce her because if he runs for president the divorce will kill him."

"You think?"

"Doesn't matter what I think. That's what he thinks."

"He talks about this?"

Adele smiled and didn't say anything.

"To you," I said. "Under, ah, intimate circumstances."

Adele continued to smile.

"Coop fools around?"

"I don't think Coop is ever fooling," she said.

"Can you talk about Gavin?"

"Un-uh," she said. "I got nothing to say about Gavin."

"Scared?"

"Prudent," she said. "Mostly he functions as Coop's bodyguard."

"Coop needs a bodyguard?" I said.

Adele shrugged.

"He's very loyal to Coop," she said.

"Do you know why Cooper needs a bodyguard?"

"No."

I nodded. Adele poured me some more coffee. She was sitting with her legs crossed, and when she leaned forward to pour, her short skirt got much shorter. My devotion to Susan was complete. I noted it merely because I am a trained observer.

"You ever hear of Darrin O'Mara?" I said.

"Why do you ask?"

"His name keeps popping up," I said.

She looked out the window for a time. Then she smiled.

"The corporate pimp," she said.

"Ah ha," I said.

"Is that what detectives say?" she said. "Ah, ha!"

"I used to say things like 'the game's afoot,' but people didn't know what I was talking about."

"And 'ah ha' is shorter," she said.

"Exactly."

"What a funny guy you are," she said. "This is one of the most successful companies in the world. Are you at all impressed with anything that goes on here?"

"Coffee's good," I said.

She smiled. "I'll broaden the question," she said. "Are you impressed with anything? Anywhere?"

"Susan Silverman is fairly amazing," I said.

"That's the woman that was with you in Chatham."

I nodded.

"Tell me about the corporate pimp," I said.

"It's just an expression," she said. "He used to spend a lot of time with Cooper and Bernie Eisen and Trent, before Trent died, and you know he's this sex guru. It's just sort of a joke around here."

"Tell me about the time he spent."

"God, you sound like one of my therapists," she said. "You know, he'd be at company social events, they'd play golf together, sometimes he'd come here to see one or another of them. They'd have lunch."

"Any women involved?"

"There were some, in those sex seminars he runs. Wives, some of our employees."

"How about Coop?" I said. "He take one of those seminars?"

"Not that I know."

"Big Wilma?"

Adele put her head back and laughed.

"Wait'll you meet Big Wilma," she said.

33

Susan and I were cooking dinner at my place, for Hawk and a thoracic surgeon. Which is, of course, to say that I was cooking dinner and Susan was setting the table, and putting cut flowers around.

The surgeon was an absolute blockbuster of a black woman named Cecile. I was making my own version of moussaka, with zucchini and onions and peppers and no eggplant. I hate eggplant. I was drinking a martini made with orange vodka while I cooked, and the rest of them were sitting at my kitchen counter drinking martinis too, and watching me.

"I hope this isn't too exhausting for you," I said while the lamb was browning.

"No," Hawk said, "I'm cool with it. But how come you didn't prepare in advance."

"I was busy fighting crime," I said.

"Who's winning?" Hawk said.

"Crime," I said.

"Little guy with the long hair reappear?"

"Not yet. I'll let you know."

"I ready to pounce," Hawk said.

Susan took so small a drink of her martini that it might simply have been that she sniffed at it.

"Something I've been thinking," she said. "When you had lunch with the CEO of that company."

"Bob Cooper," I said. "Kinergy."

"Yes. Wasn't that a private club?"

"That's why I felt so honored," I said.

"So how did Mr. Long Hair get in?"

"You're making me look bad," I said. "I never thought of that."

"As long as one of us did," Susan said.

"The finger of suspicion would point at Coop."

"I'd think so," Susan said. "Of course I'm not a detective."

"Oh shut up," I said.

Susan smiled her contented smile and took in another gram of martini vapor. I went back to my moussaka.

"Where did you learn to cook?" Cecile said. "I'm always curious about men who cook."

"We been cookin', " Hawk said to her.

"Shh," she said. "Did you learn from Susan?"

Hawk and I laughed.

"What?" Cecile said.

"If I made you coffee," Susan said, "I'd burn it."

"Oh. Then who?"

"I grew up in an all-male family," I said. "My father and my two uncles. All of us cooked."

"No women?"

"None that lived there," I said.

"So there was no stigma attached?"

"No."

The moussaka got made. The martinis got drunk. I opened some wine and we sat at the table to eat. Pearl took a position next to Hawk and poked her head in under his elbow and rested her head on his thigh. Hawk broke off a biscuit and gave it to her.

While we were eating I said, "I've got a plan."

"Oh, thank God," Hawk said.

"I need some information on a guy named Darrin O'Mara who runs, ah, sex seminars."

"Isn't he on the radio?" Cecile said.

"You listen to him?" Hawk said.

"No need," Cecile said. "I have you, Chocolate Thunder."

Hawk grinned.

"What you need?" he said to me.

"I need undercover," I said.

"At a sex seminar?" Susan said. "I'll do it."

"You've been seen too much with me," I said.

"I'll say."

"What I need is Hawk and Cecile to enroll, and see what's really up in these seminars."

Hawk looked at Cecile.

"What do you think?" he said. "Doctor Covert?"

"What are you trying to find out?" Cecile said.

"I think there's something fishy about everything O'Mara's involved in. I need information."

"I understand that," Cecile said. "But why look into these seminars?"

"Because, at the moment, I have nothing else to look into, and I hate spinning my wheels."

"And what do you expect to find out?"

Cecile was not a fools-rush-in kind of girl.

"I want to know if there's any reason for someone to refer to him as a corporate pimp."

Cecile thought about it.

"I'd be with you?" she said to Hawk.

"Every moment," Hawk said.

"And I wouldn't have to do anything I didn't want to do."

"No," I said.

" 'Cept with me," Hawk said.

"There isn't anything I don't want to do with you," she said.

I looked at Susan.

"Wow," I said, "why don't you ever say things like that to me?"

"You're not Hawk," she said.

"More deadly than the adder's sting," I said. "What do you think? Can you do it?"

Cecile looked at Hawk. "What do you think, Licorice Stick?" she said.

"Sure," Hawk said.

Licorice Stick?

34

I met Marlene Rowley for lunch at the new Legal Seafood in Cambridge. The weather was nice so we sat outside in Charles Square. I didn't know whether it meant that widowhood agreed with her or didn't agree with her, but Marlene had porked up a bit. Her face was puffy and her butt was more robust. When we were seated she had a glass of white wine. I ordered iced tea.

"Don't you drink?" Marlene said.

"I try not to at lunch. Makes me sleepy."

"Isn't that interesting," Marlene said. "It has no effect on me, you know."

She was talking to me but her eyes were ranging Charles Square. The waiter brought our drinks and took our order.

"You were taking a seminar with Darrin O'Mara," I said.

"Who told you that?" she said.

She took a large snort of white wine.

"Darrin."

"My God," she said. "That's a violation of confidentiality."

"That's what it sounds like to me," I said.

"That bastard," she said.

"So tell me a little about that," I said.

"Why?"

"Why not?"

"I don't need you prying into my sex life."

"You don't?"

"Oh don't be so smart."

"I'm trying," I said. "But I'm not succeeding. What were the seminars like?"

"Could you order me another glass of wine?" Marlene said.

"Sure," I said.

When that was accomplished I said, "What were the seminars like?"

Marlene drank from her second glass.

"They were emancipating," she said. "When I entered the program I was in thrall to sexual convention."

"Yikes," I said.

"Do you know what thrall means?"

"I do," I said.

"What?" she said.

"Captive," I said.

"Well, you are smart," she said.

"I am. But not because I know what thrall means. Tell me about escaping the bondage of sexual convention."

"That's one of the first things we learned," Marlene said. "Darrin explained that people would be uncomfortable with sexual freedom, and would denigrate it."

"Disparage," I said.

"What?"

"Denigrate means disparage."

She frowned.

"Yes," she said.

Several waiters arrived at our table with lunch.

"So what did you do to escape?" when they left.

"Darrin taught us to experience our sexuality as fully as we could."

"Not a bad thing," I said. "Did he offer specifics?"

"Specifics?"

"How were you to accomplish the experiential thing?" I said.

"Excuse me?"

"Did you, ah, spouse swap? Meet people at mixers? Hang outside of South Station and yell, 'Hey, sailor'?"

"Don't be offensive," she said.

"Sometimes it gets away from me," I said.

"Well, I am not going to sit here and talk about my most intimate experiences with you, if that's what you think."

"Isn't modesty just another snare of conventional sex attitudes?"

Marlene showed no interest in her crab salad. She snagged a busboy on his way by.

"Could I have some more wine?" she said.

"I send your waiter right over," the bus boy said.

"Why are you asking me all this?" Marlene said.

While she waited for the waiter, she tipped her glass up to drain the remaining droplets. I had a spoonful of my chowder.

"I'm detecting," I said when I'd swallowed the chowder. "Did O'Mara do anything but urge you to be free?"

"I am paying you to find out who murdered my husband," she said.

The waiter brought Marlene a glass of wine.

"You should probably bring me another glass, when you get the chance," she said to the waiter.

"Certainly, ma'am," the waiter said.

He glanced at me.

"More iced tea, sir?"

I shook my head. Marlene guzzled some wine. I had some chowder.

"Did O'Mara do anything to help free you of your Victorian hangups?" I said.

Marlene was looking around the courtyard. There might be someone important.

"What we learn in the seminar experience, and what we say and do there, belongs to us, and to no one else."

"Not even me?" I said.

She giggled and raised her wineglass toward me.

"Especially not you," she said.

The waiter arrived with the backup glass and she finished off the one she was drinking so he could take it with him.

"Did you and Trent meet Bernie and Ellen at the seminar?" I said.

"Of course not. Bernie and Trent worked together at—" She

tried to say Kinergy, but got the *G* transposed and it came out "Kingery."

She didn't seem to notice. I asked her some more things. She drank some more wine. I finished my chowder. She didn't touch her crab salad. I drank the rest of my iced tea. She had some more wine. I continued to learn nothing about Darrin O'Mara. I considered Spenser Crimestopper, Rule 2: If after repeated efforts you don't succeed, quit. I paid the check. As I was paying it, Marlene stood suddenly.

"I have to wee-wee," she said.

"Thanks for sharing," I said.

She turned from the table, and staggered and fell backward and sat hard on the brick patio with her legs splayed out in front of her. I got to her just ahead of a woman at the next table.

"Are you all right?" the woman said.

"Shertainly," Marlene said.

I got my hands under her armpits and hoisted her up.

"Shleepy," she said.

"She needs the ladies' room," I said to the woman at the next table. "I'll get her there. Can you go in with her?"

"Of course," the woman said.

I wanted to kiss her.

"But if she falls again," the woman said, "I don't think I can pick her up."

"I'll wait outside," I said. "If you need me, just sort of clear the way, and I'll come in and get her."

The woman from the next table smiled. She was a strong-looking woman with a large chest and black hair salted with gray.

"Okay," she said.

I steered Marlene toward the ladies' room, and waited outside. After a longer time than I would have thought, they came out.

"I wee-wee-d," Marlene said.

"Swell," I said.

35

I got a room at the Charles Hotel, and maneuvered Marlene up to it. She thought we were going to throw off convention's thrall, but I got her to lie down on the bed for a minute first. She fell asleep at once. And I made good my escape.

I went across the river to my office, with the intention of opening my window, putting my feet up on my desk, locking my hands behind my head, and figuring out who killed Trent Rowley. I might have sat there a long time, but fortunately when I went in the light was flashing on my answering machine. *Yea, a distraction.* I pressed the new message button.

The voice said, "Quirk. I'm on Lime Street. Something you might be interested in. You'll see the cars."

Lime Street is on the flat of Beacon Hill, old Boston. Red brick, narrow access, town houses, money. It's not a very big street, and it was easy to see the half dozen police cars, parked wherever their drivers had felt like parking them. There was crime-scene tape strung around the entrance to a four-story brick town house. The front door had one violet pane in the window. I told the uniform at the door that Quirk had called me. He nodded and yelled back into the house.

"Guy to see the captain."

There was a moment, then a voice yelled something, and the uniform ushered me in.

Another uniform said, "Captain's straight back."

I walked down the hall to the back room and into a bright room, with a lot of windows that looked out onto a tiny garden. There was a big-screen television and a music system, a wet bar and some heavy leather furniture. On the floor, face-down, was a dead man with a lot of blood on the back of his head. He was wearing a green terrycloth bathrobe. Quirk stood with his hands in his hip pockets, looking down at the body. Crime-scene people were dusting, and photographing, and shining lights. Belson stood next to a pair of narrow French doors that opened into the tiny garden. He was looking at the room. He didn't say anything when I came in. I knew what he was doing. I'd seen him study a crime scene before. He probably didn't know I was there.

"You called?" I said to Quirk.

He looked up.

"Know this guy?" he said.

"Gotta see his face."

Quirk was wearing white crime-scene gloves. He bent down and slipped one hand under the dead man's head and raised it. I squatted and took a look.

"Gavin," I said. "Security director at a company called Kinergy. Out in Waltham."

"Found your name in his Rolodex," Quirk said.

I looked down at Gavin. There was a nine-millimeter pistol on the floor a few inches away from his right hand. Behind me, Belson moved away from the French doors and began to move slowly around the room. I didn't have to look to know what he was doing. He always did the same thing. He looked at everything. Opened every drawer, picked up every lamp, moved every drape, every pillow, every seat cushion. He looked under rugs, behind furniture. The crime-scene people did what they did. Belson did what he did.

"Suicide?" I said.

Quirk shrugged.

"Bullet entered the top of his mouth," he said. "Exited the top of his head in the rear. Consistent with a guy ate his gun. Piece is a nine-millimeter, Smith & Wesson. One round missing from the magazine. Been recently fired."

"Note?"

"On his computer screen. No signature."

Quirk picked up a piece of paper from an end table near the couch.

"We printed out a copy."

He handed it to me.

I killed Trent Rowley. I accept my responsibility. But I can no longer live with it.

I handed it back to Quirk.

"Sound like him?" Quirk said.

"Hard to say."

"You involved in the Rowley thing?" Quirk said.

"I am."

I looked out into the tiny garden. There was no one there.

"Let's you and me go outside, and I'll tell you what I know."

Quirk nodded toward the narrow French doors and followed me out into the garden. There was a small stone bench next to a little pool with a miniature waterfall making a pleasant sound. The rest of the little space was flowers and herbs, and four tomato plants. I sat beside Quirk on the stone bench and told him what I knew about Gavin and Kinergy.

"I'll talk to Healy about the murder," he said. "You have any thoughts?"

"I don't have a thought. I have a feeling."

"Swell," Quirk said. "I'm a feelings guy."

"O'Mara is in this thing someplace. Everywhere I look I see the tip of his tail going around the corner."

"You think Gavin did it and felt bad, and popped himself?"

"No."

"Even though he says so?"

"Even though somebody says so."

"You think somebody else popped him?"

"I don't know," I said. "I don't know enough about him."

"I will," Quirk said. "In time."

One of the crime-scene people opened the back door.

"Captain," she said. "Something you should see."

"Come on," Quirk said, and we went back into the house.

A small bookcase against the far wall had been moved aside

and Belson was squatting on his heels. He was shining a flash-light on the wall just above the baseboard.

"Fresh patch here," Belson said. "Little one."

Quirk and I bent over. The baseboard and wall were painted burgundy. About three inches up from the baseboard was a small white circle of something that looked like joint compound.

"Could be a bullet hole," Quirk said. "Or a phone jack, or a gouge in the plaster."

"Behind the bookcase?" Quirk said. "Dig it out."

It was a bullet. Belson dug it out and dusted it off and rolled it around a little in the palm of his hand.

"There's a fireplace on the other side," Belson said. "Slug was up against the firebox."

Quirk nodded. He bent over, looking at the slug in Belson's upturned palm.

"Looks like a nine to me," Belson said.

Quirk nodded again and looked at the bookcase.

"No hole in the furniture," Quirk said.

"So the bookcase was moved."

"Or it wasn't there in the first place," Quirk said. "When the shot was fired."

"Patching compound is fresh," Belson said. "Surface is hard, but you dig in and it's not dry yet."

"So it's recent," Quirk said.

"We can call the manufacturer," Belson said. "Get a dry-through time. Then we'll know how recent."

Quirk glanced at Gavin's body on the floor.

"Can't be the bullet that killed him," Quirk said. "Unless he was standing on his head when he shot himself."

"The other slug, the one that killed him was high on the wall," Belson said. "About where it should have been."

Quirk looked at the wall where the first bullet had been dug out.

"Forensics will help us with that," Quirk said.

The three of us were quiet, looking at the dug-out bullet hole, low in the wall, behind where the bookcase had stood. Then Quirk went and sat on his heels beside the body and moved Gavin's right hand. He looked at it and looked at the bullet hole. He dropped the hand and stood.

"Let's not treat this as a suicide yet," he said.

36

Wilma Cooper was gardening in the vast backyard of her home in Lincoln.

"I always garden in the morning," she had said without looking at me. "Summers are so short."

I walked up the long curve of the driveway and across a brick patio bigger than my apartment and around to the back of the house where she had told me she'd be.

And there she was, in a halter top, an ankle-length blue denim sundress, a huge straw hat, big yellow gardening gloves, and battered brown sandals. She was, in fact, big. Tall, raw-boned, angular, with weathered skin and a pinched face that made her look worried. The gray hair that showed under her hat looked permed.

She took off her gloves to shake hands with me, and looked off to the left over my right shoulder while she did so. There was iced tea in a big pitcher on a lacy green metal table, with four lacy green metal chairs. Beside the tea was a small plate of Oreo cookies. We sat.

"I really don't see how I can be of help to you," she said. "I know little of my husband's business affairs."

"It was nice of you to make the iced tea," I said.

"What? Oh. Yes. I mean, I . . . thank you."

This was not a good sign. If she had trouble with *thanks for the iced tea,* how would she do with, *did your husband kill anybody?* I decided to be circumspect. She poured us each some iced tea.

"Terrible thing about Mr. Gavin," I said.

I drank a little of my iced tea. It was made from a mix, I was pretty sure. Presweetened. Diet. She looked at hers. Then sort of obliquely at me, and smiled vaguely. At what?

"Yes," she said after a while.

"Did you know him well?"

She thought about that for a little while. Far below us at the distant bottom of the backyard, a sprinkler went on by itself.

"Ah . . . Steve . . . was in our wedding."

"Really?"

She nodded. There was nothing else to drink so I swilled in a bit more of the ersatz iced tea.

"So you've been friends for a long time," I said.

She smiled again at nothing, and looked down the slope of her backyard.

"He was my husband's friend, really," she said.

"You didn't socialize."

"Oh . . . no . . . not really."

I took a quiet breath.

"Did you know Trent Rowley?"

"Ah, yes."

"Marlene Rowley?"

"She . . . she was . . . Trent's wife . . . I believe."

"Bernie and Ellen Eisen?"

"He worked with my husband," she said.

A full sentence. She was getting into the flow.

"But you didn't socialize," I said.

She shook her head and giggled slightly. Then she stood suddenly. Or as suddenly as Big Wilma was as likely to do anything.

"Excuse me," she said. "I have to do something in the house."

Then she turned and walked away. I watched her go. Her movements were stiff, as if she were not used to them. Was she leaving me in the lurch, or would she be back? I decided to wait it out. After all I had a whole pitcher of iced tea and a lovely platter of cookies. The circle at the far end of the sloping lawn made a fine spray full of small prismatic rainbows. A cardinal swooped past me, on his way someplace. Had it been something I said? I considered more tea and rejected the idea. It certainly wasn't my appearance. I had on my Ray-Bans, always a classic look. Extending the look, I was wearing a dark blue linen blazer with white buttons, a white silk tee shirt, a short-barreled Smith & Wesson revolver with a walnut handle in a black leather hip holster, pressed jeans, and black New Balance cross trainers with no socks. How could she bear to leave me?

She couldn't. She reappeared and walked briskly back across her patio toward me.

"Sorry," she said with a smile, "something I forgot."

"Sure," I said.

She looked right at me. Her eyes were bright and wide. She sat down and drank some tea.

"So," she said, "where were we?"

"You didn't socialize much with the Eisens."

"No."

"Lovely home," I said.

"Thank you," she said. "I was born here."

She picked up an Oreo cookie and popped it in her mouth and chewed and swallowed.

"Really?" I said.

You get a workable response, you stick with it.

"Yes, I moved here with my husband after my mother died."

"That's great," I said. Mr. Enthusiasm. "Be an expensive house to buy now."

"I could afford it," she said.

"Mr. Cooper does very well," I said.

"I could afford it without Mr. Cooper," she said. "I have plenty of money of my own."

"Family money," I said, just to say something.

"Yes. In fact my husband' s own wealth is actually family money too."

"His family or yours?"

"The business in which my husband has been so successful was once known as Waltham Tool and Pipe. My father started it after the war. When I married my husband, Dad took him into the business, and when Dad retired he made my husband the chief executive officer."

"I know it's indiscreet," I said, "to ask. But who has the most money, you or Mr. Cooper."

"Oh, God," she said. "I could buy and sell him ten times over."

She ate another Oreo.

"Did you ever meet a man named Darrin O'Mara?" I said.

"The sex man on the radio?"

"Yes."

"God no. Why do you ask? I would have little interest in anything he had to say."

"He is apparently a friend of your husband's."

"That's ridiculous," Big Wilma said. "My husband would have no reason to spend time with someone like O'Mara."

"He was apparently friends with the Eisens and the Rowleys too," I said.

"I'm not surprised," she said.

"Why?"

"Why am I not surprised?"

"Yeah."

"It's the kind of repugnant claptrap with which women like that would become involved."

"So you do know these women?" I said.

"I know what they're like," Big Wilma said.

We talked until she had eaten all the Oreos and drunk most of the iced tea.

Finally she said, "I'm sorry to be rude, but I'm developing a dreadful headache, and I simply must lie down."

"Lotta that going around," I said. "Everybody I talk to."

She smiled politely and I left. No loss. I wasn't learning anything. Driving back in Route 2, I speculated on what Big Wilma had ingested when she went inside. And whether what I saw afterward was Jekyll or Hyde.

37

The next morning when I went into my office Hawk was sitting in my chair with his feet up on my desk, drinking my Volvic water from the bottle, and reading a book called *The Teammates*, by David Halberstam.

"Did I leave the door unlocked?" I said.

"No."

"At least you brought your own book," I said.

I checked my answering machine, which displayed no messages. I got a bottle of Volvic water from the office refrigerator, and sat down in the client chair. Hawk flapped his page and closed the book and put it down on the desk.

"Me 'n Cecile went and took the weekend seminar with

Darrin O'Mara," Hawk said. "Now we feelin' sorry for you and Susan."

"Because we're hung up on monogamy."

"Exactly," Hawk said. "Darrin say we got to, ah, I believe he say, throw off our shackles, and experience our libidos unstructured and unconstricted."

"Wow," I said.

"Tha's what I thought," Hawk said.

He was deep into his *feet-do-yo'-duty* accent, which meant he was deeply scornful of his subject.

"Darrin say . . . he always encourage us to call hisself Darrin . . . Darrin say that if you fully unfettered your id, and experience passion without regard to convention or previous condition of servitude . . ."

"He didn't say previous condition of servitude," I said.

Hawk grinned.

"I jess throwed that in," Hawk said. "If you do that, Darrin say, then you still feel love and passion for one person more than any other, that be how you know you in love."

"And I been walking around all this time thinking I loved Susan without really knowing."

"Maybe you learned it," Hawk said, "when we out chasing her around out west."

"I already knew it," I said. "That's why we were chasing."

"Oh yeah," Hawk said. "I got to check back with Darrin on that. I think he pretty sure you just think you in love and don't really know."

"So, say you buy into this," I said. "You supposed to go out and chase down enough people to test the theory, or does he have a placement service?"

"He say we explore this with the other members of the class. I be swamped, a course. And Cecile say she be sort of uncomfortable starting out, so to speak, with the folks in the seminar, and was there any other way. And he say, he can also help us meet other people."

"How exciting," I said. "O'Mara tell you, or Cecile, what he could arrange for her?"

"There be a party," Hawk said. "Friday night. Invitation only."

"You be there?"

"Cecile will," Hawk said.

"You didn't make the cut, huh?"

"They 'fraid of the competition," Hawk said.

"And what if Cecile is swept up in it all, and arranges to dash off with some guy to Quincy or Nyack?"

"She be free to follow her passion," Hawk said.

"And the guy?"

"He be dead."

38

I was drinking coffee with Belson in his car parked in the lot of a Dunkin' Donuts near Fresh Pond Circle. There was a box of donuts on the console between us. The windows were down to catch the breeze from the parkway, and through the windshield we could look at the industrial fencing in front of us. Belson selected a Boston cream donut and took a careful bite. He swallowed and wiped a little of the cream filling off the corner of his mouth.

"You wouldn't want to eat one of these things on a date," Belson said.

"Frank," I said, "when's the last time you had a date."

"Me and the wife went over to Carson Beach and took a walk last Sunday."

"And did you eat a Boston cream?"

" 'Course not."

I selected a dainty plain donut.

"What's the forensic scoop on the late Gavin?" I said.

"Nine millimeter through the top of his mouth and out the back of his head. Angle consistent with a self-inflicted wound," Belson said.

"Powder residue?"

"Hands and around his mouth," Belson said.

"Anything on the suicide note?"

"Nope. Just a note on the computer screen. Nothing to tell us yea or nay."

"Dead long?"

"Around six hours before we got there."

"So around what, nine A.M.?"

"Around then."

"Who found him?"

"Cleaning lady, comes two afternoons a week. Let herself in, she thinks around two, found him like that."

"How long's it take that patching goop to dry through?"

"Eight hours," Belson said.

"That slug a nine, too?"

"Yeah. Matches the one that killed Gavin."

Belson had finished his Boston cream and was now selecting a strawberry-frosted donut with multicolored sprinkles on it.

"You're going to eat that?" I said.

"Sure."

"You got no taste in donuts, Frank."

"I must have," Frank said. "I'm a cop."

I drank some coffee.

"So it all works out nice as a suicide."

"Except for the second slug," Belson said.

He had a bite of the strawberry-frosted donut. I looked away.

"Except for that," I said.

"You thought about that?" Belson said.

"I have."

"You got a theory?"

"I have."

"You want to share it with me," Belson said, "or are you just in it for the donuts?"

"I'm thinking that somebody could have shot him in the mouth the way he was shot, and then put his hand on the gun and put the gun next to his face, and fired that bullet into the wall."

Belson nodded.

"Which would mean," Belson said, "that he had to move the bookcase first."

"Yep," I said, "which would also mean that he had to bring the patching plaster with him."

"Which would also mean that he planned this thing out pretty carefully," Belson said.

"And it might mean that he knew his way around the apartment."

"He did put that slug into the wall behind the fireplace, which meant it wouldn't go through."

"And," I said, "if he did all this, so as to get powder residue, he was probably not uninformed in these matters."

"Sort of the way me and Quirk been thinking," Belson said.

"Either of you talked with Healy?"

"Quirk," Belson said. "Staties don't have a clue."

"How's Quirk treating the thing?"

"Publicly we're wrapping up loose ends on a probable sui-cide. Internally we're thinking murder."

"And maybe it's related to the murder of Trent Rowley?"

"Yeah," Belson said. "We're thinking that it might be."

"And maybe it's connected to Kinergy," I said.

"Sure," Belson said. "And maybe it ain't."

"That covers most of the possibilities," I said.

Belson took another frosted donut from the box.

"What kind is that?" I said.

"Maple frosted," he said. "With strawberry sprinkles."

"Good Jesus," I said.

39

Matters of the Heart held its Friday mixer on a rainy night in a ballroom at the Balmoral Castle Hotel in Canton. We went in my car.

"You think I'll meet Mr. Right?" Cecile said as I slowed in front of the hotel.

"We here investigating," Hawk said.

"But won't I have to sleep with a few?" Cecile said. "Make it look real?"

"No sacrifice too great," I said.

It was raining hard. I parked under the pseudo porte cochere to let them out.

"Aren't we early," Cecile said.

"Need to be here 'fore anyone else," Hawk said. "So Spenser get a look at the guests."

"So can't we wait here?"

"Need to look around," Hawk said. "Let him know the setup."

"Well," Cecile said, "I suppose it's good, if Mr. Right shows up, he'll find me waiting."

They got out and went into the hotel. I pulled away and went around the porte cochere and parked in the front parking lot, where I could still see the hotel entrance. In five minutes my cell phone rang.

"Balmoral Castle appear to be leaking," Hawk said.

"Leaking?"

"They got barrels around, and plastic sheeting hung so's to funnel the rain into the barrels."

"Wow, the perfect setting," I said. "Where's the mixer?"

"In the back end, enter from the lobby."

"Any other likely entrances?"

"Nope. Anyone coming gonna have to come in through the lobby."

"O'Mara there?"

"He already inside with the DJ, couple of assistants."

"No guests."

"Just me and Cecile," Hawk said.

"Anyplace for me?"

"Yeah. Pub. Off the lobby, sit at the bar and you can see the door to the room. Big sign on an easel."

"I can see who turns out for the event," I said.

"If you alert," Hawk said.

"A challenge," I said.

"Better go easy at the bar," Hawk said.

I was wearing a light raincoat and a Pittsburgh Pirates baseball cap. I got out of my car into the rain and walked to the hotel with my collar turned up and my cap pulled down and my hands in my pockets. Inside, the lobby was a warren of barrels and plastic sheeting, which was having limited success in keeping the lobby dry. The rug squished with each step I took. Happily the Castle Bar was dry. I sat on a barstool and looked across the lobby at the entrance to a function room where a large sign said MATTERS OF THE HEART in red letters.

I ordered a beer, and ate some peanuts. I saw three women in summer dresses go into the function room. I ate some peanuts. A tall blond woman with an aggressive chest and tight white pants stalked into the function room. Two stunning Asian women, who might have been Vietnamese, entered in cropped pants and striped jersey tops. Cecile went in. Hawk came into the bar and sat on a stool beside me. I ate some peanuts. Hawk ordered a gin and tonic. We sat and watched the women drift in.

"I'm beginning to see why you might not have been invited," I said.

"You seen a man yet?"

"No."

At eight o'clock on the button, Darrin O'Mara appeared momentarily in the doorway. I put my hand up to my forehead and rubbed it gently as if I were tired. My forearm shielded my face. Darrin closed the double doors. Hawk sipped his drink. I nursed my beer. From the ballroom I could hear the faint sound of music playing.

"They dancing with each other?" Hawk said.

I shrugged and ate some peanuts.

40

The steady summer rain was coming hard and pleasant into my windshield as I drove Hawk and Cecile home from Balmoral Castle. Cecile sat up front with me. Hawk was in the backseat.

"There were no men, except Darrin," Cecile said, "and some thin guy with long hair. Darrin made a little speech."

"About?"

"Same crap," Cecile said. "True love cannot be compelled, but must be freely granted, and thus can only be available outside the obligations of marriage."

"Then what?" I said. "Enough with the love talk off with the clothes?"

"No. Each of us stood and introduced herself and walked the

length of the room and back, and the man with long hair filmed us with a video camera."

"Did Mr. Long Hair have on big glasses, like Buddy Holly?"

"He had on big glasses," Cecile said. "Who's Buddy Holly."

"Friend of the Big Bopper," I said. "What happens to the video."

"It will go to some men, who will choose one of the lucky girls, or maybe more than one," Cecile said. "This was a casting call."

"So O'Mara will field the requests," I said, "and arrange for the women to go see the men who requested them?"

"Nobody exactly said that, but all of us assumed it."

"See," Hawk said. "The course of true love can run smooth."

"Just requires a little organization," I said.

"Neither of you has thought of the real horror of this situation."

"Which is?"

"What if no one requests me."

"Blame racism," Hawk said.

"Yes," Cecile said. "Thank God I've got that to fall back on."

"What about the poor rejected white women?" I said. "You black people get all the breaks."

"Being white is tough," Cecile said.

"How is this for you?" I said.

"So far it's kind of exciting."

"There seem to be overtones of a slave auction," I said.

"I know," Cecile said. "And I keep thinking it ought to freak me out. But it doesn't. I guess because it's not really about race. It's much more about gender. The women are items. That's the part that would bother me if something was going to."

"Are you willing to stick with this a little longer?"

"How much longer?"

"Just until you hear from O'Mara," I said. "I'd like to hear what he proposes."

"I can do that," Cecile said. "As long as I don't actually have to show up at some motel room someplace."

"You won't. If there's a motel to be showed up at, me and Licorice Stick can do the showing up."

"Won't that be a disappointment," Cecile said.

"Not for Licorice Stick," Hawk said.

41

I sat in my office, with my feet up, and the window open behind me, while I read the paper. Then I called Healy at 1010 Commonwealth.

"I been thinking," I said.

"Well isn't that special," Healy said.

"When Gavin wanted me to go away he offered me a security job in Kinergy's Tulsa office."

"I've seen you work," Healy said. "I was you I'da grabbed it."

"We have two private eyes who were tailing principals at Kinergy," I said. "And now they've disappeared."

Healy was silent for a moment.

Then he said, "I'll get back to you."

Then I went down and got my car and drove up to Gloucester.

I found Mark Silver in a smallish house on the top of a hill on the east side of Lobster Cove overlooking Annisquam on the other side of the cove, and Ipswich Bay beyond it. We sat on his small deck looking at the water. Tomato plants grew in tubs on the deck. He offered me some iced tea. I took it.

"So why you want to know about Marlene?" Silver said.

He had a short haircut and a smooth tan and even features and teeth that seemed too white to be natural.

"You like her?" I said.

Mark was careful.

"What's not to like?" he said.

"Well, she's self-absorbed and self-important and insecure and autocratic and dependent . . ." I said.

He grinned.

"Okay," he said. "Okay. You know the beauteous Marlene."

"So do you like her?"

"No, of course not."

"She likes you."

"God knows what Marlene likes," Mark said. "She certainly has tried to get me to jump on her bones."

"And?" I said.

"I'm gay," Mark said.

"She know that?"

"Sure. I'm so far out of the closet I couldn't find my way back to it."

"And she was still after you?"

"Marlene was of the *one-good-fuck-from-me-will-cure-him* school," Mark said.

"Oh," I said, "that school."

"What's this got to do with her husband's murder?" Mark said.

"I don't know," I said. "I just keep talking to people, see if anything pops up."

"Good luck," Mark said.

I sipped some iced tea. There was a mint leaf in it.

"But you still trained her, even though she was annoying."

"I go house to house," Mark said. "I charge a lot. I'm used to bored upper-class women who think they can fuck me straight."

"Gee," I said. "Maybe I should get gayer."

"Honey," Mark said, "you're straighter than God."

I shrugged.

"But more accessible," I said. "How'd she get on with her husband?"

"He wasn't around much. She didn't talk about him much. When she did she talked mostly about him making money."

"You think they, I don't want to be corny here, ah, loved each other?"

"I think she thought he was a good provider," Mark said.

"You think she was faithful?"

"Wow, you are straight. All I know is she kept trying to straighten me out."

"She ever speak of an organization called Matters of the Heart?"

"No."

"She ever mention anyone named Darrin O'Mara?"

"No."

"What did she talk about when you were training," I said.

"How smart she was, how good-looking she was, how many men lusted after her but were intimidated, how much money she had."

"I detect a pattern," I said.

Mark grinned.

"She after you?" he said.

"Yes."

"Don't mean to pry, but was she successful?"

"You are prying, and no."

"I think she was glad I was gay," Mark said. "Then she could fail to seduce me without feeling like a loser."

"You know her late husband?" I said.

"Never met him. I was always there during the day. He never was."

"She ever talk about Bernie Eisen?"

"Nope."

"Ellen Eisen?"

"Nope."

"Anyone named Gavin? Or Cooper?"

"Like I said, Marlene only talked about Marlene and how fabulous she was."

"It doesn't seem much fun being Marlene," I said.

"Fun? God no. She's like half the women I train. They don't really care about being in shape. They just want a friend."

We talked for a while longer while I finished my tea. I learned nothing.

"Crushed mint in the tea?" I said.

"Yes. I grow it myself."

"Good," I said.

He smiled at me.

"A lot of things are," he said.

"Marlene?"

"Marlene's not one of them," he said.

42

It was maybe the first really great day of summer. Cloudless, bright, temperature about eighty. No humidity. I got to my office early, started the coffee, opened all three windows in my office bay, swiveled my chair, and put my feet up on the windowsill. There was just enough breeze to move the air pleasantly. The coffeemaker made a soothing noise until it finished. I got up and poured a cup and went back to the window. I felt like singing "Take Me Out to the Ball Game."

I heard the door open behind me and as I started to swivel back, I heard Adele McCallister say, "My God, Spenser, I don't know what to do."

I was around now, and had my feet on the floor.

"You could close the door," I said.

"Oh, of course."

She went back and closed it and came to my desk and stood.

"Gavin's dead," she said.

"Yes," I said, "I know."

"I heard it was suicide."

I nodded.

"Was it?"

"Probably not," I said.

"Oh, God. Oh my God."

I gestured toward my client chair.

"Sit down," I said.

"No. God, I . . . You have to help me."

"I will," I said.

"I told him. I told Gavin and now he's dead."

"You think the two facts are related?" I said.

"Of course, if its not a suicide, of course they are. Somebody killed him and if they killed him they will kill me."

"No," I said. "They won't."

"You have to protect me."

"I will," I said.

She went past me to the open windows and looked down at the street.

"Do you have a gun?" she said.

"Several."

"Oh my God, where am I going to go," Adele said. "I never had anything to do with anything like this before. For crissake I'm a Stanford MBA."

She walked away from the windows and went to my door and looked at it and turned and walked back to my desk and looked at it and at the file cabinet and the big picture of Susan that stood on top of it and turned back and passed me and looked out the window again.

"You're going to be all right," I said. "Sit, we'll talk."

"I can't. I . . ."

Her face reddened. She began to cry. Not a big full-out boohoo cry, but a sort of hiccup-y cry. Some tears, but not a downpour. I stood and put one arm around her shoulders and stayed with her, looking out at my corner, which was Berkeley Street where it meets Boylston. She whimpered a little more, then turned in against me and put her face against my chest and let herself do a full cry. While I waited for her to finish, I watched the foot traffic below. The girls from the insurance companies always looked especially good in their summer wardrobes. After a while she quieted and I took her by the shoulders and turned her and sat her in a client chair in front of my desk. Then I went around my desk and sat in my swivel. For dramatic effect I took a .357 Magnum from my desk drawer and placed it on the desk.

"Is that loaded?" she said.

Her eyes were red and her face had that puffy aftercrying look.

"Yes. Not much point to an unloaded gun."

She nodded.

"Can you help me?" she said.

"Of course," I said. "Even better if I know what's going on."

"Don't you see," she said. "I told Gavin and he must have investigated and they killed him."

"Who?"

"I'm not sure who they are," she said.

"Tell me what you told Gavin," I said.

"We are running out of cash," Adele said.

"Who?"

"Kinergy. We don't have enough cash to get through the summer."

"Why?" I said.

"I don't know yet," she said. "I just discovered it by accident."

"What does it mean not to have enough cash to get through the summer?" I said.

"We can't service our debt. For Christ sake we won't be able to meet our payroll."

"That's just like me being out of cash," I said.

"Same thing, on a grander scale. If Wall Street gets this the stock will tank."

"You have stock?"

"Tons."

"Other executives?"

"Tons. It was part of our compensation package. And the lower-level employees. Their pensions are mostly invested in Kinergy stock. They'll be broke."

"Why'd you tell Gavin?"

"I didn't know who to tell. Coop is mostly in Washington. He may not know. If he does know, he may not want me to know. Trent and Bernie ran things. If it's as bad as I think, Bernie won't want me to know."

"You fear reprisal," I said, "for reporting an economic fact?"

"Oh, God, yes. You don't know. How would you. You don't know what Kinergy is like. Have you ever worked in a big company?"

"U.S. Army," I said. "Middlesex County DA."

"No, no. I mean big business."

"I know what you mean," I said. "I was being frivolous."

"Oh."

"So you told Gavin what you had discovered. What did he say?"

"He said I was almost certainly mistaken, and I insisted I was not, and he said that I should keep my mouth shut about it and talk to no one until he'd had a chance to look into it. He said he'd get back to me."

"Why Gavin?" I said.

"Because I thought he was honest. I mean he's weird and you know, anal, all buttoned down and zipped up, but he is loyal to Coop, and I think he had integrity."

"And did you tell anyone else?"

"No."

"Did he get back to you?"

"I don't know. The next thing I heard was he was dead."

"And you don't know how much he looked into it, if at all?"

"No."

"But you feel his death is related?"

"Yes. Don't you? I mean I tell him something dreadful, and the next thing I know he's dead."

"Breakfast doesn't cause lunch," I said.

"What the hell does that mean?"

"The fact that one thing precedes another doesn't mean one thing causes another."

"Oh," she said. "I know all that. But do I want to risk getting killed for some fucking formal logic rule?"

"No," I said. "You don't."

43

I called an accountant I knew and we talked for a few minutes. When I hung up, I took Adele directly from my office
and moved her into my place on the first block of Marlborough
Street just up from the Public Gardens.

"I wish I could have gone home first and picked up some
things."

"Safer this way," I said.

"Could anyone have followed us?" she said when we went in
to the building.

"No."

"You're sure?"

"Yes."

I was on the second floor. We took the stairs.

"How do you know we weren't followed?" Adele said.

"I have superpowers," I said. "Later maybe I'll leap a tall building for you, at a single bound."

She smiled faintly. My wit was probably too sophisticated for her. I unlocked my apartment door and we went in.

"Do you live with that woman?"

"Susan? No I don't."

"Wow, you seemed so . . ."

"We are," I said.

"Oh." She looked around. "You live here alone?"

"I have visitation rights with a dog," I said. "She stays here sometimes."

She looked around some more.

"My God," she said. "It's immaculate."

"I'll be damned."

"I just . . . I'm sorry . . . I just assumed men living alone were pigs."

"Clean pigs," I said.

"Do you cook for yourself?"

"Myself and houseguests," I said. "You want coffee?"

"That would be nice," she said.

She sat on a stool at my kitchen counter, while I fired up Mr. Coffee.

"I'm going to need things," she said.

"Make a list," I said, "with sizes. Susan and I will get them for you."

"Susan?"

"I assume some of what you want may be intimate and I blush easily," I said.

She smiled a little less faintly. She was beginning to get her feet under her. My doorbell rang. She jumped six inches and spilled coffee on the counter.

"Omigodjesus," she said.

"It's okay," I said. "I'm expecting someone."

I went and spoke into the intercom and buzzed the door open and in a minute there was a knock on my door. I checked the peephole and opened the door and Vinnie Morris came in. Vinnie was a medium-sized guy with movements so quick and exact that I always thought of a very good watch when I saw him. His dark hair was barbered short. He was newly shaved, and wearing a dark summer suit with a white shirt and tie. He was carrying a long canvas gym bag.

"Vinnie Morris," I said. "Adele McCallister."

"How do you do," Vinnie said.

Adele said, "Hello."

"Vinnie's going to stay with you," I said.

"Here?"

"Yes."

"I . . . why?"

"To protect you," I said.

Vinnie put the bag down on my couch and unzipped it and took out a short double-barreled shotgun and two boxes of shells. Adele stared at him as if she'd seen a cobra. Vinnie put the shells on the coffee table and leaned the shotgun against the couch at the near end. Then he took an iPod and some earphones out and put them on the coffee table.

"Is he . . . ? Can he really protect me? He's not, no offense, Mr. Morris, but he's not big like you."

Vinnie was paying no attention to us. He walked to the door he'd just entered and opened it and looked out into the corridor for a time. Then he closed it, locked it, fastened the swing bolt, and peered for a moment through the peephole.

"It's Vinnie's position," I said, "that big just makes a better target."

"But is he, ah, competent."

Vinnie walked across my living room and looked out at the street for a moment.

"Vinnie is a very skilled shooter," I said.

"And . . . ah . . . loyal? Reliable?"

"You mean will he stay? Yes. Vinnie is a very reliable person. He will stay with you, and I will come by and stay with you, and a man named Hawk will come by. One of us will always be with you."

"Is Hawk his first or last name?" Adele said.

"Just Hawk," I said.

"And he's resourceful, too?"

"Infinitely," I said.

"How will I know him?"

"Vinnie or I will introduce you."

"And one of you will stay with me here, alone?"

"Yes."

Vinnie came back to the kitchen end of the living room and poured himself coffee.

"I don't . . . I wonder . . . I mean at night?"

Vinnie found some light cream in my refrigerator and added it to his coffee.

"We'll try not to be piggish," I said.

"I get a lot of sex, ma'am," Vinnie said. "I don't really need to have none with you."

Adele actually blushed. It was a good sign. She had calmed

down enough to be embarrassed. Vinnie was stirring five spoonfuls of sugar into his coffee.

"I didn't mean . . . I only . . ."

"I know," I said. "This is new for you. You can trust us. We'll take care of you. And we'll respect your privacy and your modesty and you."

She nodded and looked at Vinnie. He was sipping his very sweet coffee.

"May I call you Vinnie?"

"Sure."

"And I'm Adele," she said.

"Yeah," Vinnie said. "I knew that."

44

I went to see Quirk in his new high-tech office in the new high-tech police headquarters.

"Wow," I said. "You must be catching a lot more crooks now."

"We got so many," Quirk said, "they're asking us to slow down a little."

"I have a high-ranking employee at Kinergy that says the company is nearly broke."

"Gee," Quirk said.

"Two people from Kinergy have been shot," I said.

"One of them is Healy's problem," Quirk said.

"And the other one is yours," I said. "You think this might be a clue?"

"It might be," Quirk said. "Who's your source?"

"The source feels endangered and is in hiding," I said."I promised I wouldn't say."

Quirk leaned back in his chair with his thick hands laced across his flat stomach.

"And," he said, "you know where this source is, of course."

"I do."

Quirk swiveled his chair halfway and looked out the window for a bit.

"I known you a long time," he said. "So I know I can't scare you into giving me a name."

"Don't feel bad," I said. "I still think you're scary."

"Thanks. Got any evidence to say the place is broke?"

"Just the unsupported allegation of my well-placed source."

"Judges love that," Quirk said. "And, say it's so, and say we could prove it, how does it connect with my murder?"

"Don't you mean murders?" I said.

"Other one's Healy's. I only claim credit for out-of-jurisdiction crimes if they're solved."

"Of course," I said. "I don't know how it connects. Just strikes me that it might."

"Sure it might," Quirk said. "And what I want you to do is go right over to the DA's office and tell them you have an allegation from an unnamed source that might be a clue, and you want a warrant to examine the books of the most successful corporation in the Commonwealth."

"Didn't they donate a lot of money to the last election campaign of the current senate president?"

"I believe they did," Quirk said.

"Want me to mention your name?"

"No."

"Maybe Healy could get in there," I said.

"You can ask him," Quirk said.

"Think there's a chance?"

"No."

"Me either," I said.

"So," Quirk said. "I would say it's up to you, Caped Crusader."

"My forensic accounting skills may have corroded a little," I said.

"Lot of that going around," Quirk said.

"Still," I said, "if I blunder around over there long enough . . ."

"Maybe you'll write Hamlet," Quirk said.

45

I met Susan at Copley Place, which is a high-rise mall in the middle of the city. She was looking into a shop window, studying a manikin in a red leather pantsuit when I found her.

"I know a place would sell you a matching whip," I said.

"I'm sure you do," she said and gave me a kiss. "You have this Adele person's list?"

"Adele person?" I said. "Do I detect a hint of repressed hostility?"

"Yes," Susan said. "Do you have the list?"

I handed her the list. She scanned it like a specialist reading an X-ray. Every time I was in Copley Place I was dazzled by how successfully it avoided any regional identity. In here you could be in Dallas or Chicago or Los Angeles or Toronto or Ann Arbor, Michigan.

"Okay,"Susan said. "I can get most of this at Neiman's."

I followed Susan through Neiman's while she bought makeup and underwear and jeans and tops and hair-care products and pantyhose and a pair of fashionable tan loafers and various items of personal hygiene. While she was there she bought herself a sweater and some pants. After I had paid I had just enough left for lunch, so we went downstairs to The Palm.

"So why the hostility?" I said.

"To this Adele person?" Susan said.

"Yes," I said. "That hostility."

"She strikes me as a sexual predator."

"Sexual predator?"

"Yes."

"That seems unsympathetic," I said.

"Um," Susan said.

She had a glass of iced tea from which she took a sip.

"I mean you have often made yourself sexually available," I said.

"To you."

"Yes."

"I have the right," Susan said.

"And she doesn't."

"No."

"Maybe she'll make herself sexually available to Vinnie or Hawk," I said.

"That's her right," Susan said.

"But not to me," I said.

"That would not be her right," Susan said.

"Even if she did," I said, "I would remain steadfast."

"I'm sure you would."

"Then why do you care?"

"In one word," Susan said, "how would you describe your state of mind if I told you one of my male patients was living with me for a while."

"One word?"

"Yes."

"Frenzied," I said.

"Thank you."

I took a drink of my Virgin Mary.

"I can't ask her to leave right now," I said.

"I know."

"She'll be there for a while," I said.

"I know."

"I won't succumb to her blandishments."

"I know."

"But you're still going to be hostile?"

"Yes."

"But not to me," I said.

She smiled the luminous smile. The one that makes her whole face color, and clocks speed up.

"Of course not, my large kumquat," Susan said. "I love you."

"Even more than Pearl?" I said.

She kept the smile.

"Don't go there," she said.

46

When I got back to my apartment, Vinnie, with his coat off and a nine-millimeter Glock on his belt, was cooking sausage with vinegar peppers on the griddle part of my stove. A big pot was heating on another burner. Adele and Hawk sat at the counter watching him. They were drinking some Gray Riesling.

"On duty?" I said to Hawk.

"Vinnie's on duty," Hawk said. "Besides which, you knows I don't get drunk."

"I had forgotten that for a moment," I said.

Adele said, "Hello."

I said, "You seem to be warming to your protectors."

"I am," Adele said. "It's probably some variation of the Stockholm syndrome."

"Cecile called," Hawk said. "I told her to come over."

"She get a nibble?"

"Think so."

"When?" I said.

"Tonight."

"I think you're back on duty," I said.

"Pretty soon," Hawk said.

Adele watched us as we talked, and glanced now and then at Vinnie as he nurtured his sausage and peppers.

"Can you tell me who Cecile is?" Adele said." What you're going to do?"

"Cecile is a friend of Hawk's," I said."The rest is a little murky."

"Will it be dangerous?"

Hawk grinned.

"Not for us," he said.

The doorbell rang and Hawk went to let Cecile in.

"I've got a date," she said as she came into the living room.

"Of course you do," I said.

"What a relief," she said.

Cecile knew Vinnie. I introduced her to Adele.

"I need a drink," Cecile said.

"Martini?"

"Rocks," she said, "with a twist of orange if you've got it."

I made her the martini.

"This has been fun," she said, "like, you know, cops and robbers, an adventure. And I always knew that Hawk and you were around."

"Protect and serve," I said.

"Well, now I'm scared. I don't want to play anymore."

"No need. Tell us the deal."

"I go to an apartment on Park Drive," Cecile said, "and ring the bell for Griffin in two-B."

"That's it?"

"Yes. When someone answers I give my name on the inter-com. He buzzes me in and I go up to apartment two-B."

"Any instructions when you get up there?"

"None," Cecile said. "I assume I disrobe."

"Maybe I should go too," Vinnie said.

"Vinnie will stay with Adele," I said. "Hawk and I will come along."

"Do I have to go?"

"You have to say your name so he'll buzz you in," I said. "Then Hawk can take you away."

"And you'll go up?"

"Knock, knock," I said. "Who's there."

"What if he's watching, or he sees you through the peephole and he won't let you in."

"He's gotta come out sometime," I said.

Cecile shook her head.

"I've gotten this far," Cecile said. "I need to get you in there."

"We'll be with you," I said.

She looked at Hawk. He nodded.

"Okay," she said. "What's the plan."

We got to the Fenway at 6:30 and drove slowly down Park Drive past 137 so Cecile could get a look at it. Then we went on around to Boylston Street and parked in the parking lot of a supermarket a block over from Park Drive. It was 6:45. Cecile's appointment was at seven.

"One more time," I said. "You and Hawk will walk down Jersey Street. Hawk will stay around the corner out of sight and you'll continue on down toward the apartment. I'll walk up Kilmarnock Street and approach the apartment from that direction. Give me a little head start so I get there a little before you do. I'll stand on the front steps fumbling for my keys. You come up, pay me no attention, and ring the bell. The minute Hawk sees you ring the bell he starts down toward us. Your date upstairs can't be watching out the window because he's answering your ring. You get buzzed in and I go in with you, because I've lost my keys. I linger a moment to let Hawk in, you start slowly toward the elevator. Hawk comes in and goes up the stairs."

"What if there aren't any stairs?"

"We'll improvise" I said. "But I've been in some of these buildings. They have stairs that circle the elevator."

"Whatever the setup," Hawk said, "you won't be alone for a second."

Cecile nodded.

"Still scared," she said.

"Don't blame you," I said.

"Easier than cracking thoraxes," Hawk said.

Cecile made a try at a smile.

"Not for the crack-er," she said.

"So Hawk goes up the stairs," I said. "I get in the elevator with you. Hawk lingers in the stairwell at the top just out of sight and checks around the corner to see if there's a peephole. If there isn't, he walks down and stands beside the door. We go up. We get out on the second floor. You get out. I get out. You start down toward two-B. I look and if I see Hawk I know there's no peephole and I scoot down and stand on the other side of the door. If I don't see Hawk I stay in the elevator with the door open so it can't move and wait as you walk down and ring the bell. When the door opens Hawk and I run down the hall and barge in. You'll never be out of our sight."

"Okay," she said.

I looked at her.

"You be all right?" I said.

She nodded. I looked at Hawk.

"Cecile's looking a little tense," I said. "Do people of African heritage get pale?"

"Only through miscegenation," Hawk said.

He patted her thigh and we got out of the car.

47

There was no peephole. When Cecile knocked and the door opened, Hawk and I were standing one on each side of it.

"Cecile?" a man's voice said. "Yes, of course it is. Come on in."

I knew the voice. Hawk went in first. He moved the man down his short corridor without any visible effort, except that when they reached the end the man banged hard against the far wall. I turned to Cecile.

"You can come in," I said, "and meet your date."

She went in and I went in behind her. The man was Bob Cooper.

He said, "Spenser. My God. What the hell is going on?"

"He carrying?" I said to Hawk.

"Nope."

"Carrying?" Cooper said. "What the hell would I be carrying?"

"Can't be too careful," I said.

"I don't get this, Spenser. What are you doing here? Who the hell are these people?"

We were in a short hallway off of which the other rooms opened. There was a bedroom, a bath, a miniscule kitchen, and a living room. I gestured toward the living room.

"Sit down," I said. "We'll talk."

It was the kind of furnished apartment that graduate students rent, or newlyweds, or both. It was undistinguished in any way, except for the obviously new, and obviously expensive, big-screen TV/entertainment center opposite the brown corduroy couch.

"Absolutely," Cooper said. "I'm eager to hear what you've got to say."

Cooper sat on the couch. Cecile sat quietly in a badly painted Boston rocker in the corner nearest the door. Hawk leaned on the doorframe near Cecile. I sat in front of Cooper on a sea chest that had been painted brown and was being used as a coffee table. Cooper leaned back and rested one arm along the top of the couch. Casual. Fully at ease. A concerned CEO puzzled by the antics of subordinates.

"First," I said, there's nothing personal here. You seem like a nice fellow. Second, there's nothing judgmental. Your sex life is your business. I don't care if you have carnal knowledge of a Chevy Tahoe, as long as the Tahoe is a consenting adult."

Cooper frowned mildly and looked quizzical.

"And third," I said. "We got your ass, and it will just slow everything down if you try to pretend we don't."

"What on earth . . ." Cooper said.

"Stop it," I said. "Hawk and Cecile went to O'Mara's courtly love seminar, and Cecile, the lucky lady, made the cut and got invited to the women's mixer. O'Mara's assistant videotaped her, and you reviewed the tapes and, tastefully, picked her for an assignation."

"That's absurd," Cooper said. "I have no idea who this woman is."

"Which is why you called her Cecile when you opened the door."

"I did not. She must have misunderstood."

"None of us misunderstood," I said.

I looked at the big entertainment center. Mute and sort of threatening on the far wall.

"Hawk," I said. "You know how to work that thing?"

" 'Course not," Hawk said.

"I imagine I do," Cecile said.

"See what he's got on videotape."

Cooper said to Cecile, "You seem a nice young woman. But this is, after all, an illegal entry, and you really ought to think of your own best interests, here."

Cecile picked up the remote from the end table beside the couch and clicked on the gizmos in the cabinet, and in a moment the screen lit. She walked over and looked at some videotapes in a holder, selected one, slipped it in, clicked another gizmo, and after a moment of blank blue screen, there was Cecile drinking white wine from a piece of clear plastic stemware at the Balmoral Castle ballroom. Cecile shut it off.

No one said anything.

Then Cecile said, "The tape of me is labeled Cecile. There are also tapes labeled Marsha, Dorothy, Caroline . . . and, you get the idea."

"Play Marsha," I said.

"Don't," Cooper said.

Cecile looked at Hawk.

"Let's go to the videotape," Hawk said.

She picked up another videotape cassette. Cooper started to get up. I leaned over and put the flat of my hand on his chest and gently sat him back down. Cecile put it in, did the hocus pocus with the remote, and onto the screen came Marsha. Like Cecile she was good-looking, and like Cecile she was black. We watched her with her white wine, chatting with other women, and smiling into the camera. Then there was a somewhat amateurish cut, and we saw Marsha naked, and smiling past the camera, in what was almost certainly this living room. The camera tracked her as she walked through the hall and into the bedroom. Then another clumsy cut and there she was in bed with Cooper.

"Shut it off," Cooper said.

His voice was hoarse. Cecile looked at me, and I nodded, and she shut everything down.

"My wife," he said. "My wife can't know."

"Why don't you take a walk around, Licorice Stick," I said to Hawk, "see if you find some video equipment."

"I'm leaving," Cooper said.

He tried to stand, and once again I redirected him with the flat of my hand.

"No," I said. "You're not."

"You can't keep me here against my will," Cooper said.

"Don't be silly," I said.

He tried again to get up. I held him down. He tried to push my hand away. He couldn't.

"Coop," I said. "You got no chance."

He strained against my hand for another minute. I could see him debating whether to swing at me or not. He opted, wisely I felt, for not. Hawk came back into the living room with a video camera.

"Bedroom closet," Hawk said. "Lotta other stuff in there too."

"Video equipment?"

"Un-huh."

"And?"

"A selection of, ah, adult novelty items."

"Coop," I said, "you dog."

"Want to see?" Hawk said to Cecile.

"Oh, ick," Cecile said.

"That mean I'm all you need?" Hawk said.

"It means, oh ick," Cecile said.

Hawk grinned. Coop had assessed his position vis-à-vis fighting his way out of there, and found it not to be viable. He stopped pressing against my hand and leaned back again against the couch.

"Okay," he said. "I have an eye for the ladies."

He looked at Hawk standing beside Cecile.

"I mean, don't we all?" he said.

"Some of us don't use a pimp," Hawk said.

Coop opened his mouth and thought about what to say, and apparently thought *nothing* would be best. He looked at me. A couple of simpatico white guys. I'd understand. He and I could clear this whole thing up.

"You want to be a senator," I said. "Maybe president. A sex scandal? A divorce, almost certainly messy? With the likely negative effect all that would have on Kinergy stock?"

"Okay," he said. "You've got me by the short ones. What kind of deal can we make."

"I thought you'd never ask," I said.

"How much," Coop said, "will this cost me?"

He felt better. He was back on familiar turf. He was making a deal.

"Hard to say at this point. I want my accountant to have full access to all Kinergy's financial records."

"You mean an audit? Why?"

"I do," I said. "I understand Kinergy has a cash problem."

"Cash?"

"That's what they tell me."

"Absolutely not," he said.

"I want you to pay for the audit," I said.

"I can't do that. That's absurd."

"And," I said, "I want to know everything you can tell me about Darrin O'Mara."

"O'Mara?"

"Yep. The company pimp."

"O'Mara? I don't know anything about O'Mara," Coop said.

"That's the deal," I said. "Audit and O'Mara. Or we tell everyone everything."

"I'm not going to agree to that."

"I've already spoken with Mrs. Cooper."

"Wilma?"

"Yep."

"About what?"

"If I were you I wouldn't want her to find out any of this," I said.

"Oh God."

"My thoughts exactly," I said.

"I can't. I'll pay you. I am wealthy. I'll pay you a young fortune."

"O'Mara and the audit," I said. "Or Wilma and the press and probably the SEC and maybe the vice squad."

"Jesus," he said. "Oh Jesus, I can't. I can't."

I leaned forward a little with my hands clasped and my forearms resting on my thighs.

"Coop, darlin'," I said. "You gotta."

It was like pulling a camel through the eye of a needle. While we talked Hawk collected all the videotapes in a gym bag he found in the bedroom closet. Then he and Cecile sat and listened for a while. Then after about a half hour he stood.

"Me and Cecile got to go review all these tapes for evidence," he said.

"Me and Cecile?" Cecile said.

"Might have to watch them two, three times. Make sure not to miss a clue."

"Two or three times?" Cecile said.

"Maybe learn something," Hawk said.

"You might," Cecile said. "In fact you probably better."

"You like them feisty colored girls, too?" Hawk said to Cooper.

Cooper looked at the floor and didn't say anything. I gave Hawk the car keys and they left. As they went out of the apartment, Hawk said something to Cecile and I heard Cecile giggle.

48

It was late when I left Cooper. I caught one of the last cars to leave Kenmore Square on the Green Line, got out of the near-empty train at Park Street, crossed to the Red Line, and got on another near-empty train to Porter Square. It was almost midnight when I walked up Linnaean Street toward Susan's house. I liked the aloneness of the empty street, and the way I could hear my own footsteps.

Years of big business and years of political aspiration was a lethal combination. My discussion with Cooper felt like it had lasted longer than my police career. But, finally, I was pretty sure I'd gotten all Cooper had. It was a long time for not so much. But I had a date for the audit. And I had some idea of how O'Mara was fitting in.

The streetlights were on, but nearly all the interior lights were out in the condos and apartment buildings on either side of the street. Now and then there would be one room with a light on. Someone who couldn't sleep. Worried about money. Health. Love. Children. Someone excited. Frightened. Depressed. Bored. Someone doing homework. Someone having sex. Someone having a pastrami sandwich on light rye. Someone sitting by themselves drinking scotch whisky and watching Letterman.

The lights were on in Susan's living room. I walked up the stairs and rang the bell. In a moment the door clicked and I went in. I had just closed the front door behind me when Pearl came boiling down the stairs all long legs and flappy ears, and attempted to lap me to death. I could see Susan's legs on the top step, with the light behind her.

"You let anyone in who rings?" I said.

"I saw you coming up the street," she said.

"Sitting in the window all night hoping for me?" I said.

"You did call and say you were coming."

"Well, yes," I said. "If you want to think of it that way."

I got Pearl sufficiently under control to climb the stairs and kiss Susan. She got me a beer and herself a glass of wine and settled onto the couch beside me in her living room, wearing pink sweatpants and an oversized white tee shirt with The Bang Group printed on it in orange block lettering.

"Tell me about the love nest," she said.

I did.

Two beers later she said, "So you were able to blackmail him."

"I was."

"You are sometimes a heartless bastard," she said.

"I am, but never with you."

"That's true."

"It's all that matters," I said.

"To you," she said.

"To me," I said. "Who the hell else are we calling heartless."

She leaned over and kissed me lightly on the mouth.

"Tell me about Mr. Cooper," she said. "The lecherous bastard."

"Hard to find a place to start," I said.

"I have every confidence in you," Susan said.

"Okay," I said. "Cooper knew Gavin since they were both at Yale. After school Gavin joined the CIA and Cooper followed his destiny to the Harvard B School. They stayed friends. When he became CEO at Kinergy he felt the need of a loyal friend in a key position and hired Gavin to be chief of security."

"To be a CEO?" Susan said. "Of an energy company? In Waltham?"

"I asked him about that," I said. "He told me that he felt the whole team at Kinergy wasn't pulling together. He was getting threats from the no-dependence-on-imported-energy folks. He needed a tough guy, he said, that he could depend on, inside the company and in public. I had a sense he may have wanted some muscle behind him inside the company too, but he never quite said that."

"Was Gavin really a tough guy?" Susan said. "I mean a lot of those CIA people are simply information analysts. They never leave their desks."

"Quirk checked into him after he died. Nobody, of course, will exactly say anything, quite. Quirk says that he was probably a covert operations guy. Which would make him a legitimate toughie."

Susan smiled, and poured a little wine for herself. I still had beer left.

"Tougher than you?" she said.

"Unlikely."

"What did he think about the cash problem?" Susan said.

"He said he wasn't a micromanager. He said that was Trent Rowley's domain. After Trent bit the dust, Bernie Eisen was looking after the financial end in the interim."

"Did Cooper actually say *bit the dust?*"

"I'm paraphrasing," I said. "He also remarked that Adele, whom he liked personally, of course, was something of a man eater, and might not necessarily be reliable."

"*Man eater* was his term?"

"It was," I said. "Are you keeping a journal?"

"You can sometimes gain insight," Susan said, "listening to the way people speak."

"Have you done that with me over the years?"

"Of course."

"And your conclusions?"

"Sort of a big John Keats," Susan said.

"That would be me," I said. "Silence and slow time."

"And Cooper agreed to let your accountant in."

"And staff," I said. "Marty will need help."

"Did he know anything about the special whatsises, or the funny accounting?"

"He said he didn't."

"Do you believe him?"

"I think he was focused on being senator, and positioning

himself for the presidency, and that Kinergy, having made him rich, was now merely a base. I think he had little interest as long as its profits kept growing and its stock kept soaring, which made him look good."

"So Adele is right," Susan said. "He let Rowley and Eisen run the company."

"I'd say so."

"How about the O'Mara stuff?"

"Cooper met O'Mara through Trent Rowley, he says. He, Cooper, is of course totally devoted to his lovely wife, Big Wilma . . ."

"He didn't call her Big Wilma," Susan said.

"I'm paraphrasing. He's totally devoted to Big Wilma. Their marriage has been, of course, blissful, but . . ."

"Any children?"

"One son. A career Marine."

"Really? Isn't that sort of odd. I mean from a family like that."

"Probably," I said. "But despite how swell Wilma is, and how happily married they are, Coop felt perhaps there was a way to enlarge his life experience and blah and blah and blah."

"So he decided to take a seminar with Darrin O'Mara."

"He did. The Eisens and the Rowleys brought him to one."

"Not him and Wilma."

I smiled.

"You should meet Big Wilma," I said.

"Out of place?" Susan said.

"Like a mongoose at a cobra festival."

"But isn't that O'Mara's rap? Freeing husbands and wives from the bondage of monogamy?"

I shrugged.

"In Coop's case it was hubbies only. Under pressure, he did allow that not only had he an eye for the ladies, but he had eyes for African American ladies in particular, which Big Wilma is not, by the way. And, because he's so decent a guy, and trying to preserve his wonderful marriage, and in order never to em- barrass Wilma, or in any way imply a lack in her, he arranged for O'Mara to begin supplying him with the black women of his dreams."

"What a guy," Susan said. "Whose apartment is it?"

"Coop says it belonged to Gavin, who let him use it."

"You believe him?"

"No. I'm sure Gavin rented it for him. But I don't care if he lies about stuff like that. If you let a guy like Cooper weasel on the small stuff, he thinks he's winning some of the battles, and it's easier to get the big stuff out of him."

"Did others at Kinergy use O'Mara?"

"We know Rowley did, and Eisen. Coop thinks that prob- ably some other executives were involved, but he doesn't know who."

"You think that's a lie?"

"Probably."

"But you don't care."

"I'm not the sex police," I said. "I just want to know who killed Trent Rowley."

"God, I almost forgot that was what you were hired for."

"I try to keep track," I said.

"Did Cooper have anything to say about the long-haired man?"

"Not really. Said he was a friend of O'Mara's and because

O'Mara asked, Cooper had his secretary call and get the guy into the dining club."

"Does he know the man's name?"

"Doesn't remember. Says his secretary might know."

"And when the man just sat there at the bar, you don't think Cooper wondered?"

"If you want to be president, and there's a guy who knows about you what O'Mara knew about Cooper . . ."

"You don't ask," Susan said.

I nodded.

"So why would this friend of O'Mara's be following you?"

"Worried about what I might find out about Kinergy?"

"Why would he care?"

"Well, he is the corporate pimp," I said.

"I suppose," Susan said. "Do you really think that's all it was?"

"No," I said. "I don't."

"Do you know what else it would be?"

"Not yet," I said.

49

Marty Siegel came to my office carrying a pigskin attaché case and looking like he was on his way to an inauguration.

"Are you sure you're an accountant?" I said.

"I am the best accountant in the world," Marty said.

"I know that," I said. "But you're supposed to be geeky and wear glasses and a pocket protector."

"Would contacts cover me?" Marty said.

"Accountants don't wear contact lenses."

"And if they're any good they're not hanging around with you, either," Marty said. "Be glad I'm atypical."

Marty put his pigskin attaché case carefully on the seat of one of my client chairs and sat just as carefully in the other one. He was tall and lean with long black hair that waved back over his ears. He wore a black silk suit, a white shirt with a Windsor collar, and a white silk tie. His face was clean-shaven and pefectly tanned. He even had a little cleft in his chin.

"I've arranged for you to do a full audit at Kinergy," I said.

"Access to the site?"

"Yep."

"Nothing off limits?"

"Nope."

"No time limitation?"

"Nope."

"You have something on the CEO?"

"Yep."

"Good," Marty said. "What I've seen so far, they could use a good audit."

"You already know things?" I said.

"Of course," Marty said. "Would I be the world's greatest CPA and not know anything yet?"

"Whaddya know?"

Marty looked at my coffeemaker. The pot was nearly full.

"You got coffee made?"

"Yes."

"Gimme some," Marty said.

I handed him a cup and he got up and poured himself coffee and sat down and crossed his legs, making sure to adjust his pants at the knee so the crease wouldn't bag.

"Any publicly held company," Marty said, "is required by law to make quarterly and annual financial filings. The quarterlies are called 10Qs and the annuals are 10Ks."

"Isn't that something?" I said.

"You wanna learn something or not?" Marty said.

He drank some coffee.

"Hey, this stuff isn't bad," he said.

I nodded modestly.

"The filings are public. You can go to the SEC website and look them up. What you'd be especially interested in, if you were a really amazing CPA instead of some kind of semi-legal thug, would be three documents. The balance sheet, the income statement, and the statement of cash flow."

"I resent being called a semi-legal thug," I said.

"Okay," Marty said. "Illegal thug."

"Thank you."

"Any good accountant can learn a lot from those documents," Marty said. "And the great ones, like me, know to pay close attention to the footnotes."

"So whaddya know?"

"You know what mark to market accounting is?"

"No."

Marty looked pleased.

"Do you know what cost, or as it is sometimes known, accrual accounting is?" he said.

"Also no."

Marty leaned back and drank some coffee and got himself more comfortable in my chair.

"And," I said, "if you begin to tell me in any detail I will jam you into your attaché case."

"You wouldn't understand detail anyway," Marty said. "Say you kept a ledger, which in your case is unlikely, but say you did, and say you're making knuckle knives. You sell one to Hawk for a buck, and you debit your asset column one dollar, and credit your liabilities column one dollar. The two columns are always supposed to be equal."

"I don't have a ledger," I said.

"I know," Marty said. "And if you did, the columns would never be equal. But this is hypothetical."

"And Hawk's already got a knuckle knife."

"Shut up and listen," Marty said. "So you keep your ledger and somebody says how much money you got and you say a buck, and they say show me, and you take the buck out of your pocket and wave it under their nose."

I nodded. We'd get there eventually. Pushing him wouldn't do any good. Marty was one of those guys who knew so much about a thing that he had to tell you far more about it than you ever wanted to know.

"But," he said and paused.

"But?" I said.

I knew he was pausing for dramatic effect, I might as well help him enjoy it.

"Suppose you and Hawk have a deal. He'll buy a knife every year for five years. So you debit a buck from the asset side, and you credit five bucks on the liabilities. Because that's what the deal's worth over time."

I nodded.

"Get it?" Marty said. "See the problem?"

"What if Hawk dies or backs out of the deal?"

"Yes," Marty said.

He was thrilled.

"Or somebody comes by the first year and says show me the cash?" he said.

"I take out my one dollar," I said.

"And suppose the guy that's asking has just fixed your sink and seeing that you had five dollars in revenue, does it for credit, and now he wants his five smackers."

"I don't think I've heard anyone say *smackers* since I dumped all my Perry Como albums."

"Never mind that," Marty said. "What I described in grossly oversimplified terms is another kind of accounting called mark to market."

"Thank God for the gross oversimplification," I said.

"And here's a little embroidery," Marty said. "Say you think the cost of knuckle knives will go up over time, so you, or probably I, at your behest, because you pay me a monstrous retainer every year, and I am in your pocket, make a projection of how much the price will rise, and decide that they'll be worth two bucks, five years hence."

"Hence," I said.

"Yeah, hence. I went to the fucking Wharton School, remember. So now you've got a deal worth ten simoleons, and you credit that. But how much actual cash you got?"

"A simoleon," I said.

"See?"

"Is that what's going on at Kinergy?"

"I believe so."

"And the advantage of that is that it inflates your revenue?"

"Yes."

"Which makes your stock worth more?"

"Yeah, and if you need to show an even bigger profit you can just move the curve."

"Predict that knives will sell for two-fifty," I said."And then I can show a credit of twelve-fifty."

"Exactly."

"And it's legal."

"Sure, mark to market is perfectly legal, often useful, sometimes necessary, in companies where a reasonable curve can be projected. But it's less, ah, less appropriate for a company like Kinergy, whose product may fluctuate wildly because of war, or climactic events, or political decisions, or economic circumstance, or the death of some Arabian sheik."

"And you might find yourself with a cash-flow problem."

"Yeah. You have to pay your employees, for example, in cash. If you have debt to service, and if you're cash poor, you have to service that in cash. And you have to do it now, not five years from now."

"So," I said. "Worst case?"

"You can't pay your bills. You go bankrupt."

"Is that what's going on at Kinergy?"

"Might be," he said. "It seems to me that they should be showing more loss and less profit than the 10Qs are reporting."

"You think someone's cooking the books?"

"Something's going on," Marty said.

"When you do the audit," I said, "can you find out what it is?"

Marty looked at me as if I had just said something in Greek.

"Am I the world's best CPA?" he said. "Of course I am. If there's chicanery, will I find it? Of course I will."

"That's a relief," I said.

When I woke up in the morning on the couch in my living room, I could hear my shower running. At least Adele was clean. I put on my pants and had coffee made and orange juice squeezed when she strolled out of my bedroom with her hair in place and her makeup on.

"God," she said. "Coffee and orange juice waiting. What a husband you'd make."

"This morning my accountant, with the blessing of Bob Cooper, begins his audit at Kinergy."

"Really? I can't imagine."

"I think we should go over there and be handy if he wants to talk with you."

"Your accountant?"

"Yes. Marty Siegel."

"To Kinergy?"

"I'll be with you," I said.

"You think it's important?"

"Yes."

"Will Vinnie come with us?"

"Sure," I said.

"I guess that will be okay," she said.

I took my turn at the shower. There were several pairs of highly impractical-looking ladies' underwear drying on my towel rack. I tried not to blush. As I was getting dressed, Vinnie showed up for work.

"You know a skinny little guy with long hair and big glasses?" Vinnie said.

"I do."

"He's got your place staked out."

I walked to the front window.

"Corner of Arlington," Vinnie said. "Across Marlborough."

I saw him. He was wearing a blue seersucker suit, and his hands were jammed into the side pockets.

"Might be staking out Emerson College," Vinnie said.

"Nope," I said. "It's me."

"Want me to buzz him?" Vinnie said.

"No, we'll leave him alone, see what he does."

I took my coffee to the window and watched Long Hair while I called Hawk on his cell phone.

"Where are you?" I said.

"Not your business," he said.

"What are you doing."

"Very not your business," he said.

"Oh that," I said. "Long Hair's showed up in front of my house, corner of Marlborough and Arlington. Blue seersucker suit. Big glasses with black frames."

"Okay," Hawk said. "Lemme finish up here."

"Make it quick."

Hawk laughed.

"Person I with don't want that."

"Whoops," I said. "Well, do your best and call me when it's over."

"Be over already, you hadn't called me up in the middle," Hawk said. "I'll call you when I'm on him."

It was a large orange juice and two coffees before Hawk called.

"Got him," he said.

"Okay, long leash," I said. "Let's just see where he lives, who he is, that sort of thing."

"Sho," Hawk said.

With Long Hair behind us we walked to my car. I could see that it was annoying Vinnie.

"How 'bout I just put one in his foot, or maybe a knee?" Vinnie said.

"No," I said. "Gratifying though it would be."

"Are you talking about shooting that man?" Adele said.

"Yeah."

"Why is he following us?" she said.

"That's what I think we'll find out," I said. "Hawk's behind him."

Adele started to turn her head.

"Don't look," Vinnie said, and she froze.

"Wouldn't see him anyway," I said. "I expect we won't see him until he's through tailing Long Hair."

"So how do you know he's there?"

"He said he was there."

"But . . ."

"Hawk never says something ain't so," Vinnie said.

"Never?"

"Nope."

I beeped the power locks on my car doors. Vinnie opened the passenger door in front and Adele got in. Vinnie got in the back and I drove.

"So you want this man to follow us," Adele said.

"Yes."

"What if he doesn't have a car."

"Then he's really an amateur," I said. "But it doesn't matter if he follows us or just goes home. Hawk will find out who he is."

Vinnie was turned in the backseat, looking out my back window.

"He's got a car," Vinnie said.

In my side mirror I could see a yellow Mazda Miata pull away from where it was parked by a hydrant.

"Nice car for a tail job," I said.

"Blends right in," Vinnie said.

"And you think Hawk is somewhere behind him?"

"Yep."

"And after this man eventually stops following us and goes home, Hawk will follow him there and find out who he is?"

"Yep."

"What if Hawk loses sight of him or something?"

In the backseat, Vinnie laughed.

Adele turned and looked back at him.

"Well, it's certainly possible, isn't it?"

"No," Vinnie said, "it ain't."

51

Kinergy provided us what they called a liaison executive, a slightly overweight currently blond woman in a dark blue suit named Edith, and put us all into a vacant office. I knew how it came to be vacant. It was Gavin's. Marty had brought two helpers with him. The helpers were women, and good-looking. In the years I'd known Marty, all his helpers had been women, and all of them had been good-looking. It made me wonder sometimes about the nature of the hiring interview.

Marty commandeered the desk that used to be Gavin's. The helpers set up their laptops on a conference table that had been moved in. Marty suggested Adele pull a chair up to the desk and join him. She did. Vinnie headed for the outer office.

"No," Adele said. "Please, Vinnie. If you could stay."

Vinnie said "Sure" and sat at the end of the conference table and looked at nothing. Marty smiled at Adele. She smiled back.

"Tell me what you know," Marty said.

Since my job was simply to ensure compliance, I decided to take a break from the complexities of accounting and went and sat in the outer office at one of the empty secretarial desks. I was a bit big for the armless secretarial chair I was in, but there weren't any others. I put my feet up on the secretarial desk and made do.

I was still there with my feet up and my hands laced comfortably across my stomach about ten minutes later, when Bernie Eisen came in with a couple of other suits he didn't identify.

"What the hell is going on here," Eisen said to me.

"Audit," I said.

"Audit?" Bernie said. "An audit? Whose audit? Who's auditing us."

"Me."

"You? You? You can't audit us."

I didn't hear a question there, so I didn't answer it. Eisen looked past me to the inner office.

"Who the hell is he?"

"Marty Siegel," I said. "World's greatest CPA."

"Adele and Edith are both in there," he said.

"True," I said.

"For God's sake, what is Adele doing in there?"

"Talking to the world's greatest CPA," I said.

"Get her out of there," he said to the two suits.

The two suits looked puzzled.

One of them, a sturdy-looking curly-haired guy who reeked of health club, said, "Get her out?"

"Get her out," Eisen said. "If she won't come, goddamnit, drag her."

The suits looked even more uncertain.

The health-club guy said, "Bernie, we can't just drag somebody."

The other suit was balding and tall and looked more like cycling and tennis than health club. He shook his head and kept shaking it.

"God knows what she's telling him," Bernie said. "I'm getting her out of there."

"Bernie," I said. "See the guy at the end of the conference table? The one sort of half asleep looking at the ceiling?"

"What about him?"

"I fear that if you touch her he will shoot you."

"Shoot?"

"Vinnie is very short-tempered," I said.

Bernie stared at me for a moment.

Then he said to the health-club suit, "Get security up here."

"I think you should consult first with your CEO," I said.

"Coop?"

"The very one."

Bernie stared at me, then he nodded the cycle/tennis guy toward a phone on the desk beside my crossed ankles.

"Call Coop," Bernie said.

The suit dialed a number.

"Bernie Eisen," he said after a moment. "For Bob Cooper."

He handed the phone to Bernie.

"Coop?" Bernie said after a moment's wait. "Goddamnit,

Coop, you got any idea what's going on down here in Gavin's old office?"

Bernie listened silently for a moment.

"Well, I think you need to get down here," Bernie said.

He listened again.

"No, Coop. Listen to me. You need to come down."

He listened.

"Okay," he said and hung up.

I smiled at him. He turned away from me. The two suits stood without purpose near him.

"You guys may as well go back to work," Bernie said. "Coop and I will deal with this."

"You want security up here, Bernie?"

"No. Just go ahead back to work."

Bernie stood and stared in at Adele as if he could somehow impale her on his gaze. We were quiet until Coop swept in.

"Spenser, great to see you," he said and stuck out his hand.

After I shook it, Coop turned to Bernie and put a hand on his shoulder.

"Bernz," he said, "I'm sorry. I understand your concern and it's my bad that I didn't give you a heads-up on this."

"You see Adele in there?" Bernie said.

"Adele is fine. We have nothing to hide here, Bernie, that I know about."

"Coop," Bernie said. "That's not the point. We have nothing to gain from this. There's no good in it for us to have some quite possibly hostile entity rummaging around in the way we conduct our business."

"Oh, come on, Bernzie. Don't get your knickers all twisted. I welcome any inquiry into any aspect of Kinergy's operations. I believe that the inquiry will simply underscore the fact that we run one of the great companies. And, however unlikely, if there is something amiss, no one wants to know it more than I do."

"Coop . . ."

"Bernz," Cooper said, and his tone became a little harder. "I have authorized this audit."

Eisen took a breath and held it and let it out slowly. Then he turned without a word and walked out. Cooper grinned at me.

"Don't mind Bernie," he said. "He cares a lot about this company."

"He cares a lot about something," I said.

Coop grinned harder.

"Anything you need," he said, "you just let Edith know. And if there's any problems, send them straight to me."

"Right," I said.

Coop was so enthusiastic it was easy to forget that he was being blackmailed into this.

Susan joined us for dinner at the new Davio's in Park Square.

"Did you see that man follow us back from Kinergy?" Adele said.

Vinnie nodded.

"Did you see Hawk?"

Vinnie shook his head.

"How do you know he's there?" Adele said.

Susan smiled.

"He's there," Vinnie said.

"But how do you know?"

"We know," Vinnie said.

"We do?"

Vinnie nodded at me.

"Him and me know."

Adele looked at Susan. "What is this?" she said. "Some sort of secret society?"

"Yes," Susan said. "That's exactly what it is. Full of unsaid rules and regulations which none of them will even admit to knowing."

"Is it just the three of them?" Adele said.

"No," Susan said.

She looked at me.

"Who else is a member?" she said.

"This is your hypothesis," I said.

"Okay," Susan said. "Well, there's some cops. Quirk, Belson, a detective named Lee Farrell; the state police person, Healy."

Susan took a ladylike slug of her Cosmopolitan.

"And a man named Chollo from Los Angeles, and a man named Tedi Sapp from Georgia. Anybody else?"

"Bobby Horse," I said.

"Oh, yes," Susan said, "the Native American gentleman."

"Kiowa," I said.

"Kiowa, of course," Susan said.

"Little dude from Vegas," Vinnie said.

"Bernard J. Fortunato," I said.

"See," Susan said, "if you lull them into it they'll admit to the existence."

"And what are you," Adele said, "that you know all this, den mother?"

Susan laughed and had a little more of her pink drink.

"I'm scoring the club president," she said. "Gives me special status."

"So why are they so certain that Hawk is where he said he'd be?"

"Because he's like they are," Susan said.

"And they'd be there?"

"If they said so."

"And," she nodded at me, "does he ever tell you why they're all like that?"

"They don't know they're like that," Susan said.

"What do you two think of what she's just described?" Adele said.

"I think I'll have some linguine," I said.

"Veal looks nice," Vinnie said.

"Don't even bother," Susan said.

Adele took a long breath. Susan was glancing around the room, and her glance stopped and rested.

"Excuse me, there's two people I really want to see."

She got up and walked two tables down from us where a slim dark-haired man was having dinner with a slick-looking woman. Susan kissed them both, and spoke with them in high animation. Susan in high animation is like watching a big-screen re-release of *Gone with the Wind*: all the color, all the drama, all the excitement. Adele and I watched her. I was drinking beer. Adele and Vinnie were sharing a bottle of red bordeaux. Vinnie wasn't watching her. Even as he sipped his wine Vinnie was looking at everyone.

When Susan came back to the table, I said, "Who's that guy you were kissing?"

"Tony Pangaro," Susan said. "I'm surprised you don't know him. He's been involved in every major real estate development east of the Mississippi River since the Spanish American War."

"Gee," I said. "He doesn't look that old."

"Exaggeration for effect," Susan said.

"Fair's fair," I said. "Can I go kiss his date?"

"No."

We ordered dinner. Vinnie ordered another bottle of wine.

"Marty tells me the audit is progressing," I said to Adele.

"Yes. He seems like such a smart guy."

"He said you've been very valuable."

"Good," she said. "I'm glad. He's awfully nice."

"In a sort of sharkish kind of way," I said.

"Sharkish?"

"Exaggeration for effect," I said.

Vinnie sampled the second bottle of bordeaux and nodded and the waiter poured some for each of us.

"Now that the whistle has been blown," I said to Adele, "and the audit's under way, there really isn't any danger to you anymore."

"Oh, no, I still want to stay at your place," she said.

"There's no reason for anyone to kill you," I said. "Unlike Gavin, if that's what happened, it's too late to prevent you from talking."

"Please," Adele said. "If I move back home, at least let Vinnie stay with me for a while longer."

"That would be up to Vinnie," I said.

All three of us looked at Vinnie. He was drinking some wine. He finished, put the glass down, and shrugged.

"Sure," he said.

Adele looked at Susan.

"Do you think it will be all right?"

"If he says it will be all right," Susan said, "it will be all right."

Adele nodded slowly, looking at Vinnie.

"Susan," she said, "you sound like the rest of them."

"She is," I said. "Wait'll she shows you the secret handshake."

53

Hawk showed up in my office just before noon with several sandwiches in a bag. He took one out and handed it to me.

"Six grams of fat," he said. "I figure, I eat enough of these and I get to do one of those commercials."

"Hawk," I said. "You were born with two percent body fat, and you've trimmed down since."

"So we lie to them."

"We?"

"I thought you might want to get in on it," Hawk said.

"I'll eat a couple and see if my belt feels loose."

"How 'bout coffee," Hawk said.

"I made a fresh pot," I said.

"When?"

"Yesterday."

"Be fine," Hawk said.

I poured us two cups and opened one of the sandwiches.

"Long Hair's name is Lance Devaney," Hawk said.

"Lance Devaney?"

"What it say under his doorbell."

"I bet he wasn't always Lance Devaney," I said.

"Probably not," Hawk said. "He lives in the South End, on West Newton Street."

My sandwich was pretty good. I ate some more of it.

"Two-unit town house," Hawk said.

"That so?" I said.

I had known Hawk too long. He was building to something.

"Doorbell on the other unit say Darrin O'Mara."

Hawk never showed anything, but something in the way he sat back a little and took a bite of his sandwich spoke of self-satisfaction.

"Darrin O'Mara," I said.

"Un-huh. So I stick around outside there and I wait and, you know, O'Mara got that seven-to-midnight talk show, so about two-twenty in the morning here he come, lippity lop."

"Lippity lop?"

"Authentic African argot," Hawk said. "I is trying to educate you."

"Lippity lop."

"Yeah, and in he goes right next door to Lance."

"Now that I think of it, I wonder what name Darrin O'Mara was born with," I said.

"I stuck around for maybe another hour and no sign of life so I moseyed on home."

"Not lippity lop?"

"I mosey," Hawk said.

"Of course."

I picked up my phone and dialed Rita Fiore.

"Could a paralegal get me the owner's name at a couple addresses in the South End?" I said.

"If I tell him to," Rita said.

I asked Hawk the address.

"Both units?" he said.

"Both."

He gave them to me and I told Rita.

"Who are you talking to?" Rita said.

"Hawk."

"Hawk is right there with you?"

"Yes."

"Oooh!" Rita said.

"Oooh?" I said. "Among criminal lawyers you are generally considered the queen piranha. And I mention Hawk and you say 'oooh!'?"

"I am still in touch with my girlish side," Rita said. "I'll call you back. Please tell Hawk *kiss kiss* for me."

I hung up. Hawk was unwrapping a second sandwich.

"Wow," I said. "You look slimmer already. Rita says to tell you *kiss kiss*!"

Hawk smiled as if to himself.

"Have you and Rita ever . . . ?"

Hawk looked at me blankly. I didn't pursue it, because the phone rang. I picked it up.

"So quick?" I said.

"So quick what?" Healy said.

"Sorry, I was expecting someone else."

"I found the missing private eyes," Healy said.

"In Tulsa?"

"Yep. Gavin arranged for them to get security jobs at Tulsa Kinergy. A Tulsa detective talked with them. They admit the jobs seem like a boondoggle."

"They shed any light on anything else?"

"Not yet. Tulsa's going to talk with them some more, and let me know."

"And you, grateful for my help, will, of course, let me know."

"If I'm not so grateful I choke up," Healy said and broke the connection.

"The missing private eyes," I said to Hawk. "Being overpaid and underworked at the Kinergy Tulsa facility."

"Gavin arrange that?"

"I guess he made them an offer too good to refuse."

"Wanted them out of town."

"I assume," I said. "So we wouldn't find out he'd hired them to spy for him."

"And he done that why?" Hawk said.

"My guess is he got wind of the wife-swapping sex stuff that was going on with O'Mara and was trying to find out what was going on so he could protect Cooper."

"Maybe Gavin not so bad a guy," Hawk said.

"Maybe."

We drank some more coffee. Yesterday's fresh coffee isn't as good as today's fresh coffee, but it is far, far better than no coffee.

"I am only a simple hooligan," Hawk said, "and you the detective. But I notice every time we run down some sort of lead it connect us to O'Mara."

"Keep thinking like that," I said, "and maybe you can be a detective."

This time when the phone rang it was Rita.

"The two town houses on West Newton Street," Rita said, "are both owned by Darrin O'Mara."

"Any mention of anyone named Lance Devaney?"

"Lance Devaney?"

"Um-hm."

"Of course not," Rita said.

"Okay," I said. "Hawk says *kiss kiss*!"

"You're lying to me," Rita said.

"Yes, I am," I said. "But with the best of intentions."

She hung up.

"O'Mara owns both units," I said to Hawk.

Hawk slid into a British public school accent.

"By God, Holmes," he said. "This bears looking into."

"It do," I said. "Perhaps you could stay on Lance Devaney for a while longer."

Hawk stayed with his Holmesian accent.

"Be interesting," he said, "to establish the precise nature of their relationship."

"You're thinking they might be more than friends?"

"Happens sometimes," Hawk said.

"Happens quite often," I said, "in the South End."

"Be kind of cute," Hawk said, "champion of courtly romance turns out to be Oscar Wilde."

"All kinds of love," I said.

"For sure," Hawk said. "And what do you think happens to Matters of the Heart if O'Mara turns out to be homosexual?"

"Might broaden his audience base," I said.

"Might."

"Or everything might go right into the tank," I said.

"Might."

"Why don't you look into it," I said.

"I believe I will," Hawk said.

54

I was part of the family at Kinergy by now. I smiled at the woman at the reception desk and headed for the elevators without anyone saying *may I help you*. Kinergy was humming right along, just as if things were going good. Up in Gavin's old office Marty Siegel and his two assistants were deep into their computers. Adele sat close to Marty, I noticed, looking over his shoulder. Vinnie sat tilted back in a high-backed leather swivel chair near the window. He shot me with his forefinger when I stuck my head in the door.

"Progress?"

Marty didn't even look up from the computer.

"You'll be the first to know," he said.

"Attitude?" I said. "After I got you this lucrative gig?"

"Go track down a criminal," Marty said.

"Okay," I said.

Adele smiled at me, though I think Marty had replaced me in her affections, or Vinnie, or maybe both. Inconstancy, thy name is Adele.

I went on down the hallway to Bob Cooper's big corner office and past the platoon of secretaries in his outer office to the desk of the secretary in chief in her inner office. And she ushered me into the vast digs of the CEO. Cooper stood when I came in and gave me a huge smile. Welcome wherever I went.

"Spenser," Cooper said and came around his desk, which took him a while because the desk was nearly the size of Vermont. "Good to see you. You caught any bad guys lately?"

"You should know," I said

"Ouch," Cooper said. "I really walked into that one."

I sat in one of the eight or ten red leather armchairs scattered around the office.

"Talk to me about Gavin," I said.

"Ah, Gav," he said. "Damn shame. Was it definitely decided it was suicide?"

"If it wasn't," I said, "why would someone kill him?"

"God," Cooper said, "you think someone killed him?"

"Well, if it wasn't suicide, what would be the other options?" I said.

"Of course! Jesus, I'm getting dumber by the minute," Cooper said. "Do you think it was murder?"

"Do you think he would kill himself?" I said.

"No, Gav was a stand-up guy. He'd been in the military, you know. And then he was CIA. It's hard to imagine he'd kill himself."

"So who would kill him?" I said.

"The police think it's murder?"

"Police haven't told me," I said.

There was no special reason to lie about it, but on the other hand there was no special reason not to.

"Gav would have been hard to kill."

"Depends on who's got the gun," I said.

"Yes, of course, I suppose with a gun . . ."

"So why would someone shoot him?" I said.

"Well, he was in that spy business, he might have made enemies."

"I'd buy that more if he wasn't the second Kinergy guy in a month to die of gunshot."

Cooper nodded. On the oak-paneled wall behind his desk was a huge portrait of Big Wilma, looking pretty much like Big Wilma.

"I suppose," he said.

"Any other thoughts?"

"I don't . . . I can't . . . everybody liked Gav."

"He was very loyal to you," I said.

"Oh God yes. I mean Gav and I go way back. Ever since Yale."

"He wasn't married," I said.

Cooper smiled. "Gav wasn't good with women," Cooper said.

"Which means?"

"He was divorced three times."

"Any current action?" I said.

Cooper grinned at me, man to man.

"There was always current action for Gav," Cooper said.

"Any current favorites?"

"Gee," Cooper said, "I don't want to be telling tales out of school."

"Neither do I."

He recognized the threat. It almost pierced the jovial CEO shield for a moment, but he righted himself.

"But I'd rather tell them than have you tell them," he said. "Gav was spending a lot of time with Trent Rowley's missus."

With all the information clutter, I had forgotten it: my first meeting with Jerry Francis, outside the Rowley home:

"So far the only person I caught her with was him."

"Her husband?"

"Yeah. Guy who hired me."

Gavin had hired him.

"Gavin was seeing Marlene Rowley?" I said.

"Yep." Cooper smiled some more. "No accounting for taste, I guess."

"I guess," I said.

I'm just going out for my walk," Marlene said. "Can you walk along with me?"

I said I could, and we set out. Marlene was in full stroll regalia as we walked past the big empty lawns of her neighborhood. A symphony of spandex. At the end of her street we turned and walked along the seawall. Below us the ocean washed across the beach. There were people in bathing suits down there and occasionally one worth studying. Marlene made no reference to getting fried and passing out on me the last time I saw her. I suppose, in fact, that there isn't so much to be said.

"Shame about Steve Gavin," I said.

"Yes."

"Did you know him?" I said.

"Oh, yes, of course. I saw him at a number of Kinergy functions that I attended with my husband."

"Would you have any idea why he might want to kill himself?"

She couldn't resist the dramatic opportunity. She did an amateurish impression of someone thinking. Frowning, her lips slightly pursed, her eyes narrowed.

"Maybe he was unlucky in love," she said.

"Who was he unlucky in love with?"

"Who? Oh God, I don't know. I just said that. I mean, isn't that why a lot of people kill themselves?"

"Any reason someone might want to kill him?"

"Someone? Who? I thought he killed himself."

"Well," I said, "just hypothetically, if it wasn't suicide but murder. Who would you suspect?"

"Suspect?"

"Hypothetically," I said.

A good-looking woman walking a small black-and-white bull terrier walked past us. I glanced at the woman's backside. Excellent. Marlene looked at me as if she disapproved.

"Cute dog," I said.

"I can't really guess," Marlene said, "even hypothetically, about Mr. Gavin's death. I barely knew him."

I nodded. We walked along the water. Ahead of us on the sidewalk a couple of gulls were fighting over an orange peel. They flew up as we reached them and came back down to continue the fight when we were past.

"Marlene," I said, "you were intimate with Gavin."

"Excuse me?"

"Marlene," I said, "you were intimate with Gavin."

"That's a terrible thing to say."

"Marlene, you really should stop lying to me," I said. "A private detective named Jerry Francis spotted you together several times. A very reliable source, highly placed at Kinergy, says Gavin was keeping company with you."

Marlene stopped and leaned on the iron railing along the seawall and stared out at the ocean. Then she turned slowly back toward me. Her eyes looked a little moist, but some people can produce that look with effort.

"Damn you," she said. "You leave me nothing. No shred of dignity."

"Maybe a shred," I said. "Tell me what you can about Steve Gavin."

"He was a very fine man."

"And you're heartbroken by his demise," I said.

"Oh, why must you be cruel. I couldn't show what I felt."

"Why not?"

"I was a, a married woman," she said.

"Until your husband's death."

"And after my husband's death?" she said. "What would people think if the next day I was flouncing around with Gav?"

"Hideous to contemplate," I said. "Did Gav have a theory about your husband's death?"

"No, of course not, he would have told the police immediately."

"I'm sure," I said. "Did he know anything about your wife-swap arrangement with Bernie and Ellen?"

She slapped me. It was a showy slap, but not a very hard one. I stayed on my feet.

"I'll take that as a no," I said. "Did he know about Darrin O'Mara and his program?"

"You bastard," she said. "Doesn't anything touch you?"

"I'd be deeply touched," I said, "if you told me whether Gavin knew about O'Mara and his program."

"I may have mentioned something about it."

"Did you tell him you were involved?"

"No, of course not. I simply told him that I'd heard it was popular at Kinergy."

"Was he interested in that?"

Marlene was doing defiant now. Her head was up and sort of tilted back, as one's head would be if speaking to an underling.

"Yes. He seemed quite interested. It is, after all, quite an interesting concept."

"You bet," I said. "Was there anything else he was interested in?"

She almost blushed.

"I don't mean that," I said. "Was there anything else about your husband or about the company that Gavin seemed interested in."

"There was some sort of money problem, I think. He had talked with Trent about it, I think, before Trent passed away."

"Did he say what kind of money problem?"

"Nothing I paid attention to. I found it all very boring."

"Did he talk with anyone else about it?"

"He seemed worried about Coop," she said. "After Trent's tragic death, Gav said maybe he could talk with Bernie."

"Bernie Eisen."

"Yes."

I put my hands up to defend my face.

"He didn't know about you and Bernie."

She had moved from haughty to icy.

"I told you, no."

"So how long had you and Gavin been an item?" I said.

"Since, let me see, we were, um, together for the first time . . . it was just a little while before Trent's death, I believe."

The woman with the bull terrier came back along the seawall toward us. I watched her over Marlene's shoulder. The front was as good as the back.

"So for a while there," I said to Marlene, "you were juggling Trent, Bernie, and Gavin. Pretty good."

"I wasn't juggling anything," she said. "I was trying to find myself."

"How'd that work out?" I said.

"Very well, thank you. I know who I am now."

I avoided the trap she had set. I did not ask her who she was. Whoever she was I was sick of her. The only genuine thing she had done since I met her was to get zonkered at lunch.

"Shall we walk back?" I said.

"Tired already? I always walk five miles. I'm in excellent condition."

"Can you do a one-armed push-up?" I said.

"A what?"

"Never mind," I said.

"Five miles too much?" she said.

"Yes," I said. "I'll say goodbye here."

"Well, I hope I've been helpful," she said.

"Sure have."

"Good," she said. "We always enjoy our time together, don't we."

"Always," I said.

56

Back at my office I called the management company that ran the Park Drive apartment complex where Coop had his love nest, and impersonated a police officer. There was no one named Cooper in the building, nor anyone named Griffin. Apartment 2B was rented to Steven Gavin. Checks were from his own account.

I looked at the big picture of Susan on my filing cabinet.

"So," I said to her, "Gavin knew about the love nest, and he knew about something else, something to do with money which he'd spoken to Trent Rowley about, and maybe Bernie Eisen."

And Trent Rowley was dead, and so was Gavin. Had he mentioned the money thing to Cooper? Didn't sound like it. Why not? Because Cooper wasn't involved in the hands-on day to day. Because he wanted to be president and would need deniability if some sort of money scandal emerged.

"So why was Gavin having Marlene and Ellen followed?" I said to Susan's picture.

Susan's picture didn't seem to know, either. And why, in addition, was he pursuing an affair with Marlene? Love was of course a possibility. But it wasn't a certainty. The fact that he was having her followed wouldn't be a problem if he wanted to sleep with her. Jerry Francis and his partner reported only to him, and they thought he was Marlene's husband anyway. And she was attractive enough to sleep with if you didn't have to talk with her afterward. Maybe he slept with her because she was available. But he went back, if I could believe her, for more. Why? Research?

Say he was as loyal to Cooper as Adele said he was. Cooper seemed to think so, though I detected no real sense of loss. Cooper probably didn't feel much about people other than Cooper. And say, because he was renting the love nest for him, that Gavin knew Cooper was involved in some sort of seamy sex thing. But he might not have known what, and it worried him. He wanted Cooper to be a senator, maybe president, too.

But the seamy sex thing wouldn't get him killed. Cooper would know he could keep the secret. Hell, Cooper had him rent the apartment on Park Drive. So it was something else. And the only something else I knew about was the money thing. Which Marty was working on. So why was Gavin having two wives tailed about a money thing?

I looked at my picture of Susan again. It had been taken in the country, and she was wearing a straw hat and holding a glass of wine, and talking to someone off camera and smiling, like she smiles, with her head turned and tilted a bit. She was so Susan in the picture. It was my favorite.

"What am I missing?" I said.

Susan's picture gave it some thought. I gave it some thought. Neither of us said anything for a while. It was a humid August. Outside my window it had gotten darker than it should have in the middle of the afternoon. And I could hear thunder. The thunder wasn't close. Too far away yet for lightning. No rain yet. But the air was suspenseful with it, and it would be here soon.

Then I said, "They intersect."

I was pretty sure Susan's picture said, *of course they do.*

There was something in common between the seamy sex thing and the money thing. Otherwise I could make no sense of it. Which meant here came Darrin O'Mara again. And his pal Lance.

57

I went over to police headquarters and sat with Belson. Neither Devaney nor O'Mara had a record. So we looked at pictures. We looked at pictures of people with long hair and big glasses. I didn't see Lance. We looked at pictures of people who had the initials L. D. and D. O. and didn't find Lance or Darrin. We looked under first names. We looked under last names. We tried under sex scams. Extortion. Shooting incidents. Every possible cross reference we could think of. Neither of them was there.

"Maybe if I had the kind of clout that a sergeant of homicide had, I could get the radio station to help us with O'Mara's background."

"And what do you think the station will say first?" Belson said.

"Freedom of speech. Freedom of the press. Freedom from unwanted search and seizure. Freedom to misinform us about the weather and almost everything else."

"And if I cut through all that and we get something," Belson said. "What issues will come up in court?"

"Freedom of speech," I said. "Freedom of the press. Freedom from unwanted search and seizure. Freedom to misinform us. Freedom to sell advertising. . . ."

"So forget the station. Anything we want to find out we have to have a persuasive reason to be asking."

"Even if it wasn't evidence that would hold up in court," I said. "If I knew something about him, I could find a way to get him."

"From what you told me maybe we could get him for pimping," Belson said.

"Couple things wrong with that," I said. "He gets paid for his seminars, which are legal. Hard to prove any more than that."

"How about the broads he sends out to clients. He doing that because he's a fool for romance?"

"Almost certainly not," I said. "But to prove he's doing anything worse than running a dating service and calling it something else, we'd have to force a lot of people to testify who don't want to."

"And ruin the reputations," Belson said, "of people who didn't do anything worse than get laid."

"Lot of us guilty of that," I said.

Belson grinned at me.

"Thank God," he said.

"So we don't want to do that," I said.

"Probably not," Belson said.

"Of course O'Mara doesn't have to know we don't want to do that."

"That's right," Belson said. "He doesn't."

"I'll keep it in mind," I said.

"Here's another thing to keep in mind," Belson said. "So far you haven't told me anything much that this guy is guilty of that matters much. You got any reason to think he murdered anybody?"

"I know."

"You holding back?"

"Of course I'm holding back," I said. "But nothing that would change what you know."

"So why do you think he's a suspect?"

"Because," I said, "I suspect him."

Belson nodded.

"Thanks for clearing that up," he said.

By the time I got out of Police Headquarters the thunder had arrived and the lightning and rain were with it. The rain was nearly overwhelming the windshield wipers. The traffic was crawling. The thunder was close and assertive, followed almost at once by the lightning, which gleamed like quicksilver on the wet cars and slick streets. It was almost seven when I got back to my office. I was just hanging up my raincoat and shaking the water off my hat when Hawk came in, wearing a black silk raincoat and no hat. He was carrying something in a plastic grocery bag.

"Glorious feeling," Hawk said.

He took off the raincoat.

"Laughing at clouds," he said.

He went to my closet and opened the door and got a towel and dried off his gleaming head.

"So high up above," he said.

"Stop it," I said.

Hawk shrugged.

"Just being cheerful," he said. "You got any food?"

"I'll call for a pizza," I said.

"Two," Hawk said.

He went to my office refrigerator and took out two bottles of Stella Artois and handed me one.

"You got anything to tell me?" I said.

"Darrin and Lance," he said. "The love that dare not speak its name?"

I drank some beer.

"This will give rise to considerable speculation on our part," I said.

"I thought it might," Hawk said. "That's why I wanted two pizzas."

"I'll get right on it," I said and reached for the phone.

58

I took a slice of green pepper and mushroom pizza and bit off the triangular point.

"So what do you know?" I said.

"Nothing you can use in court," Hawk said.

"Nothing to prove in court," I said. "I just need to know."

"They're a couple," Hawk said. "They have dinner together. They go to the movies together. They take evening strolls together. They go food shopping together."

"Doesn't mean they're intimate," I said.

"People see you and Susan together," Hawk said, "they know you intimate. They see me and you together they know we not."

"And thank God for that," I said. "But I see your point."

"Couples be different together than friends," Hawk said.

"They ever affectionate in public?" I said.

"Nope."

"But you're sure?"

"Yep."

Hawk stood up and went to the refrigerator and got us two more beers. The plastic grocery bag was still on the floor beside his chair.

"What's in the bag," I said.

Hawk smiled widely.

"Hopin' you'd ask," he said.

"I fought it as long as I could," I said.

"So today," Hawk said, "I'm staying dry in a doorway across the street, and the two lovebirds come out with an umbrella, which confirm my suspicion that they gay."

"Real men don't use umbrellas."

"Exactly," Hawk said. "And I see that they going just down the block to a fancy restaurant. So I drift on down there and look through the window and they just sitting down. I watch for a minute and the waiter give them each a big dinner menu. He take a drink order and when he leaves they start reading their menus. So I think to myself they gonna be an hour, more likely two, which give me time to look around."

"So you hotfooted it back to their place," I said.

"Ah don't 'hotfoot,' " Hawk said. "Ah moved rapidly but with grace to their place and entered."

"Any trouble getting in?"

"Haw!"

"So you found something," I said.

"I did."

"And it was a plastic grocery bag," I said.

"That's what I found to put it in," Hawk said.

"Resourceful," I said.

Hawk put down the pizza slice he had in one hand, and the bottle of beer he had in the other. He picked up his plastic grocery bag and took out a leather-covered scrapbook. He placed it gently on my desk and leaned back and revisited the pizza and beer. "Found it in the bottom drawer of Lance's bureau," Hawk said. "Under his shirts. Nice shirts. Too small, though."

"You were thinking about stealing his shirts?"

"Sure. But they too small for either of us."

"Good of you to think of me," I said.

I opened the scrapbook. On the first page was a newspaper clipping from the *Kansas City Star* for March 10, 1991. It described the murder of a Kansas City couple. The next page was the *St. Louis Post-Dispatch* for January 1992, a prominent doctor found murdered in his car in a parking lot in Belleville, Illinois. And so it went. Nine murders in all, full press coverage, neatly clipped and pasted into the scrapbook. Murder number 8 was Trent Rowley. Number 9 was Gavin.

"Lance is a creepy guy," I said.

"But a very nice dresser," Hawk said.

"He finds this missing he'll scoot," I said.

"Probably ain't the first thing he checks when he comes home," Hawk said.

"When he does look he'll be gone," I said.

"Turn it over to Quirk?" Hawk said.

"Doesn't prove he did the murders, only that they interested him."

"Still be enough for them to bring him in, wouldn't it? Fingerprint him. Maybe find out who the hell he is?" Hawk said.

"Or maybe they don't and all they got is the scrapbook, and no judge will admit it as evidence, since it was the result of an illegal search by a notorious felon. And they have to turn him loose."

"Notorious felon?"

"Well known," I said.

"And proud," Hawk said.

"You find a gun?"

"No."

"You toss O'Mara's place?"

"Yep."

"You didn't have time to pull everything apart."

"Nope."

"So we know all this about him," I said. "And we don't know who he is."

"You figure he done them killings in each city that he's got clippings from?" Hawk said.

"Yeah. We can give Quirk a list of the murders, let him see what he can find out. But it'll take time."

"Might be able to lift some prints off the cover too," Hawk said.

"Might," I said. "But I don't want to give it to them yet."

"Because you want to hit him with it."

"Sometime," I said. "If I need to."

"We could go over to the house they share, right now," Hawk said. "And return the scrapbook and ask them about it, and see what happens."

"If we were lucky Lance might take offense," I said.

"And go for his gun," Hawk said. "And we wouldn't have to look for it no more."

"Tempting," I said. "But not yet. Stay on Lance awhile longer. I want to see what Marty Siegel digs up. There's a connection here someplace, and I want to know what it is."

"After a while," Hawk said, "you sort of forget why you got hired, don't you?"

"I still haven't found out who killed Trent Rowley."

"And if you did, and it was some stranger, had nothing to do with all this, would you quit?" Hawk said.

I smiled.

"I'm a curious guy," I said.

"You surely are," Hawk said.

"Don't lose Lance. Even if you have to let him know you're there, don't lose him."

"Remember to whom you are speaking," Hawk said.

"And keep in mind that Lance has probably killed nine people."

Hawk grinned. "I got him there," Hawk said.

"I'm sure you do."

59

"It's Byzantine," Marty said.

"You find it Byzantine?" I said.

"Me, the world's greatest CPA. I'm in awe."

"Is it legal?" I said.

"Oh, God no," Marty said.

"Can you explain it to me?"

"I can oversimplify it drastically," he said.

"Oh good," I said.

The rain had broken the humid stretch and the day was dry and pleasant. Marty had an office on Staniford Street, and we'd agreed to meet sort of halfway between us. Which is why he and I were sitting on a bench in the Common, not very far from the Park Street Station, watching the street life move past us on Tremont Street. Pigeons and squirrels circled us in case we were interested in feeding them, which we weren't. But neither a pigeon, nor a squirrel, is easily discouraged.

"As far as I can tell, your culprits are Trent Rowley and Bernie Eisen. Do you know what a special purpose entity is?"

"No."

"A special purpose entity is a device often used for securitization of debt."

"I urge you to oversimplify," I said.

"It was always my intention," Marty said. "Say you have a shop, Spenser's Sandwich Shop. You have a bunch of customers who buy their sandwiches on credit, for which convenience you charge them one percent a month. So at the end of the day you have earned a hundred bucks plus one percent a month. But there's nothing in your cash register. What you do is, you create a special purpose entity, and call it, say, Susan's Equity Trust. You can invest your own money in this company, but at least three percent of it has to be independent capital. Then you sell your hundred dollars worth of accounts receivable and its interest payments to Susan's Equity Trust. Now at the end of the day you have a hundred in cash. Susan's Equity Trust, in turn, sells shares in itself to investors eager to make one percent a month on the sale of sub sandwiches. So Susan's gets a markup. The investors get their money back in installments plus the one percent interest. Got it?"

"Yeah, sure, banks do that, with mortgages, don't they? Car dealers?"

"Lot of people do it and it's perfectly legitimate."

"Even when banks and car dealers do it?"

"Amazing but true," Marty said.

"But in the case of Kinergy?"

"Rowley and Eisen were creating SPEs to hide debt. Remember what I told you. They had a ton of earnings, but not much cash."

"The old mark to market accounting trick," I said.

"Very good."

"So the absence of cash would begin to create debt."

"Right again," Marty said. "Or one or another project was a losing proposition."

"And payment on the debt would use up cash."

"It would."

"So they needed to keep these matters off the books, or their profit picture would suck and people would stop buying their stock."

"Gracelessly put, perhaps," Marty said, "but not inaccurate."

"And the SPEs were their solution."

"Better," Marty said. "They could sell one operation or another, that had a lot of debt, to the SPE and show it on their books as income."

"And that's legal?"

"Remember what I said about conditions?"

"Essentially that the SPE needed to be independent of the creating company."

"Yep. These weren't. They were owned mostly by Rowley and Eisen, or Mrs. Rowley, or Mrs. Eisen, people like that. And the money they raised to create the SPEs was guaranteed by Kinergy stock."

"Including the three percent?"

"Yes."

"So they weren't independent of Kinergy."

"Nope, and, as they developed, some of these outfits began to have interests antithetical to Kinergy's, but very beneficial to Rowley and Eisen. You want to hear how?"

"Jesus Christ, no," I said. "I never want to have this discussion again."

"Which is why you are not a world-class CPA."

"Thankfully," I said. "Isn't there somebody supposed to approve stuff like this?"

"Board of directors," Marty said.

"They approved?"

"The Kinergy board of directors, as far as I can see, would have approved compulsory pederasty if urged by Trent and Bernie."

"Isn't there any outside accounting?"

"There is, one of the best accounting firms in the Northeast. Kinergy pays them about three million a year."

"So much for them," I said. "And where was our man Coop in all of this?" I said.

"Yonder somewhere gazing at a star," Marty said.

"You don't think he knew?"

"I don't think he wanted to know. A company like Kinergy is out there on a shoeshine and a smile. The way they do business they have to increase earnings every year, so their stock will look good and the investment banks and big brokerage will suck around them."

"So he looked the other way?"

"I don't think he even had to," Marty said. "These deals are very complicated. The flowcharts look like they were created by Hieronymus Bosch. I had trouble figuring some of it out."

"Holy mackerel," I said.

"And," Marty said, "Coop's probably not that smart."

"And him a CEO," I said.

"Disheartening, isn't it," Marty said.

"Is there trouble ahead?"

"For Kinergy? You better believe it," Marty said.

"Are they going to go under?"

"Absolutely," Marty said. "And pretty soon."

"Any indication that Eisen knows this, or Rowley did?"

Marty smiled at me.

"They both owned tons of Kinergy stock," he said.

"How nice for them," I said.

"Rowley was selling it as fast as he could without causing a stir. Eisen still is."

"A lot of money?"

"Yes."

"A hundred dollars?" I said.

"No. That's a lot of money to you. A lot of money to them is millions."

"Millions?" I said.

"Depending on the price of the stock, quite a few millions."

"So it would be in their best interest to keep pumping Kinergy up until they unloaded their stock," I said. "Then they can let it flop."

"Most of the employees' 401(k)s and other pension vehicles are invested in Kinergy stock."

"So when it tanks?"

"They're fucked," Marty said.

"You CPAs talk a language all your own," I said. "You happen to run across the name Darrin O'Mara anywhere?"

"Sure. He owns one of the SPEs."

"How about Lance Devaney?" I said.

"Yep."

"SPE?"

"Yep."

"Funded in one way or another by Kinergy?"

"Yep."

"Hot damn," I said.

"Hot damn?"

"Yeah," I said. "Detectives talk a language all their own, too. Can we prove all this stuff in court?"

"If I can continue to access the books," Marty said. "We going to court?"

"I have no idea," I said.

60

Marty headed back toward Staniford Street and I sat on the bench for a while after he left. From where I sat I could see down Tremont to where the Eisens had their condo. In front of me a lot of black and Hispanic kids were heading down Winter Street toward Downtown Crossing. There was a little police substation down there. One of the cops told me once that the ghetto kids gathered there, not to make trouble but because it was safe.

This was new. I had information overload. Usually my problems went the other way. I knew that they were all in it, whatever *it* quite was, and whoever *they* quite were. We had a lot of money and a lot of sex, much of it adulterous. The top two motives. I knew the names of all the players. I knew who was getting the money and who was getting the sex. Within reason I understood what was wrong at Kinergy and what Rowley and Eisen were doing about it—they were taking the money and scuttling down the mooring lines. All I had to do was figure out which one of them killed Rowley and Gavin, and I was there. Wherever *there* quite was.

Assuming that Lance Devaney's murder scrapbook indicated something more than lurid fandom, he would be a nice choice. He'd be a better choice if I could suggest why he killed Rowley and Gavin. Gavin probably got shot because he got too close to something, whatever the *something* quite was. But why did Rowley get shot? My head felt overtaxed. I was thinking too much about too much and concluding too little. I wasn't used to it. I was much more adept at thinking too little and drawing conclusions from no information. I sat for a while and updated my ongoing survey of tightness trends in women's clothing. While I sat, a hard-nosed rodent with a ragged tail that spoke of battles won paused in front of me and glared at me for peanuts. There are some macho squirrels on the Boston Common. I needed a fresh and intelligent perspective on all this. It was quarter to two in the afternoon. Susan would be free at five. If I took my time over a late lunch, and was leisurely getting across the river, Susan would be almost through. I could go upstairs at her place and maybe have a little nap with Pearl until Susan was ready to enjoy my discussion of SPEs. I stood up. The squirrel with the ratty tail reared onto his hind legs.

"Don't push it," I said to the squirrel, "I'm packing."

61

Wouldn't Eisen seem a suspect?" Susan said. "Two people in a criminal enterprise, and one dies, isn't his cohort a logical possibility?"

We were sitting on her front steps watching whatever walked down Linnaean Street. Pearl sat between us. Alert.

"He would be if he got something out of killing Rowley."

"What could that be?" Susan said.

"I can't find a way that it would be money," I said.

"Weren't they involved with each other's wives?"

"Yeah. But as far as I can tell it was 'you bop mine and I'll bop yours.' No need for jealousy."

"Unless one of them wasn't as mutual as the other."

"Marlene thought that Rowley was serious about Ellen Eisen," I said.

"And Ellen?"

"I saw no sign of that."

"Still, jealousy is possible."

"Seems so old-fashioned and American a motive for this tangle of vipers."

"But possible," Susan said. "What else would there be in it for Eisen to kill Rowley? Don't focus on the case, just think of possibilities. Why would one conspirator kill a coconspirator?"

"Silence," I said. "Rowley was going to blow the whistle and Eisen knew and killed him so he wouldn't."

"So we have jealousy as a possibility," Susan said, "and silence as a possibility."

"He might kill him to get his share, but I can't see how that would have worked. And an investigation of the death might uncover the situation at Kinergy before Eisen had unloaded all his stock."

"So that probably isn't a possibility."

"No," I said. "Probably not. I sort of like the silence theory."

"Something makes it resonate?"

"Gavin," I said. "Gavin was almost certainly killed to shut him up."

"Ahh," Susan said.

"I love it when you say shrink things," I said.

"And when I don't," Susan said.

"True."

"Does Eisen strike you as a man who would kill people?"

"He's a yuppified, corporate jerk," I said. "And we both know the range of people who might kill someone . . . but no. He doesn't strike me so."

"Is there anyone who does strike you so?"

"Lance," I said.

"If the scrapbook means what you think it means. People do collect fetish objects, you know."

"Yeah, but assuming he's just a fetish object collector isn't useful to the project," I said.

Susan smiled at me.

"Good heavens," Susan said, "a variation on Pascal's wager."

"So assume he's a serial killer who keeps his notices," I said, "he'd make a first-rate candidate."

Susan thought for a minute. Pearl eyed a man and woman walking by in funny hats. Her whole body stiffened with the desire to bark at them. Mine too. But we had both been urged repeatedly not to, and we were both practicing restraint.

"Or maybe you could partner him with your other candidate," Susan said.

"How so?" I said.

"Well, you have two members of a criminal enterprise," Susan said, "one of whom maybe has reason to murder but not the will; and the other of whom has no reason to murder, but, maybe, plenty of will. Makes kind of a nice fit, doesn't it?"

I nodded. Pearl put her head on my thigh and I patted her.

"I'd have thought of that in another minute," I said.

"Of course you would have," Susan said. "You're a trained detective."

"And don't you forget it," I said.

Pearl looked worried.

"You think I might be right?" Susan said.

"I do."

"So have we solved your case?"

"We have, if we can find a judge and jury that will convict on your say-so."

"Oh, that. Don't you just hate having to support a theory?"

"Supporting theories, little lady, is my middle name."

"Really?" Susan said. "How odd."

62

I sat most of the next day in my office with my feet up drinking too much coffee and looking out my window and thinking. I made some phone calls late in the afternoon, and at about 6:15 I stood with Hawk in the shelter of a doorway on West Newton Street across from where Lance and Darrin lived. It was raining again.

"They're still in there."

"They are," Hawk said."Should be having supper together."

"Which condo?"

"O'Mara," Hawk said.

"Okay, I got an appointment with Bernie and Ellen Eisen at seven-thirty," I said.

"Wouldn't want to be late," Hawk said and we went across the street.

The rain was hard, one of those humid weather downpours that usually don't last long, but also don't usually solve the humidity. It had to do with a high or a low or an occluded or a nimbus cloud or something. We got into the shelter of the tiny doorway. I was looking at the bell listings.

"Ah took the liberty of having some keys made," Hawk said. "Be on my expense report."

"You don't have an expense report," I said.

"Well, if I did, it be on it," Hawk said and opened the front door of O'Mara's town house and went in. I could hear classical music playing on a good sound system.

"Bach," Hawk whispered. "Brandenburg number three."

"So you say," I whispered.

The living room was to the right and past that the dining room. I could see O'Mara and Lance at dinner. There were candles, and a bottle of white wine in a bucket. They were both wearing coats and ties, as if they had dressed for dinner. When we came into the room, both men sat frozen for a moment, staring at us. The CD player was on a shelf next to the door. I shut it off. Lance put both his hands in his lap. I saw Hawk smile gently to himself. He walked around the table and stood near Lance.

"How did you get in here?" O'Mara said. "What on earth do you think you're doing?"

"We need you at a meeting," I said.

"Meeting? What in God's name are you talking about?"

"We need you to come to a meeting with Ellen and Bernie Eisen," I said.

"Don't be absurd," O'Mara said. "We're not going any-where."

"Ah but you are," I said. I took hold of the back of his jacket with both hands and lifted him out of his chair. He almost screamed, and his voice broke when he said, "Lance."

With a quick movement in his lap Lance took out a nine-millimeter pistol. As he tried to cock it, Hawk took it away from him with his right hand, got a fistful of Lance's long hair with his left hand, and yanked Lance sideways out of his chair and stood him up.

"Gonna be the right caliber," he said to me, and dropped the nine into the side pocket of his raincoat.

Lance tried to hit him but Hawk held him at arm's length and Lance couldn't reach. He kicked at him without much success. He bit at Hawk's forearm. Hawk hit him with a six-inch right-hand punch and Lance went limp. Hawk let go of his hair and Lance sank to the floor.

"I hate biting," Hawk said

"Oh god," Darrin said. "Oh God, oh God, oh God."

I let him go and he threw himself onto the floor covering Lance with his body.

"Oh God," he said, "oh God."

After a moment Lance began to move a little and after an-other moment he sat up.

"He'll be okay," I said. "He just got his bell rung."

"Give him back his gun," O'Mara said to Hawk, "and we'll see how tough you are."

"Loyal," Hawk said to me.

"Nice trait," I said.

"Don't see much of it," Hawk said, "anymore."

"Get him on his feet," I said to O'Mara. "We need to get going."

"You can't just come in here," O'Mara said, "and, for God's sake, kidnap us."

"Sure we can," I said. "Let's go."

"Now," Hawk said.

O'Mara got Lance onto his feet. He looked at Hawk and made an odd reptilian noise. It was more than a hiss and less than a snarl, and it oozed out of him as if he didn't even know he was making it.

"Hum a little more of that," Hawk said. "Maybe I know the words."

Lance's eyes were very wide and round-looking, and his breathing was shallow and rapid and the nasty sound kept oozing. O'Mara had his arm around him and was whispering to him as we walked close together out of the town house and through the rain to the hydrant where I was parked. O'Mara got in back with Lance, with his arm still around him. Hawk got in front beside me and turned and rested his arm on the back of the seat and looked at O'Mara and Devaney. This time there was a silvery .44 Magnum revolver in his right hand. Nobody said anything. I started up, turned on the wipers, took a right onto Columbus Avenue, and went across the wet city.

By the time we circled the Common and got to the Eisens' building on Tremont, Lance had stopped making his reptilian sounds, though his breathing was still shallow and fast. He had not, as best I could tell, stopped staring at Hawk. Hawk, as best I could tell, didn't much care. Bernie and Ellen answered our ring together at their front door. When they saw O'Mara and Devaney they tried so hard to have no reaction that it was a reaction.

"I'll tell you right now," O'Mara said when we were inside and sitting in the living room, "they forced us to come here with them."

"Forced?" Bernie said.

"They hit Lance. The black man hit Lance."

Hawk smiled at Ellen.

"Kinda liked it," he said.

Lance hissed again. But briefly.

"Bernie?" Ellen said.

"What the fuck," Bernie Eisen said, "is going on here."

"Funny you should ask," I said.

63

We had ourselves arranged in the living room. Hawk was leaning against the wall near the door with his raincoat still on but unbuttoned. I was on a straight chair, turned around so I could lean my forearms on the back of it, like the cops in film noir movies. Ellen and Bernie were on a couch. Darrin and Lance sat in matching wing chairs set at a slight decorator's angle on either side of the window through which you could see such a great view over the Common where not long ago Marty Siegel had explained special purpose entities to me. I was more comfortable now. I understood this kind of thing better.

"Here's an interesting thing," I said. "Hawk and I have consistently acted in a high-handed, indeed, quite probably illegal manner, both at the O'Mara home earlier this evening, and here in your lovely condo high above the city."

No one said anything. Lance was giving me the death stare with his little reptilian eyes. The stare would have made me more nervous if Hawk hadn't taken his gun.

"And no one has mentioned calling the cops," I said. "Seems odd."

No one said anything.

I had Lance's scrapbook in a manila envelope. I picked it up off the floor by my feet and opened it and took out the scrapbook. I opened it to the pages devoted to Rowley and Gavin, leaned around the back of my chair, and placed it faceup on the coffee table where all of them could look at it. Everyone looked at it. No one spoke. Lance licked his lips once.

"We found that in Lance's shirt drawer, which, incidentally, Hawk, who is clearly fashionable, tells me is filled with handsome shirts."

"What is it?" Ellen said.

"A scrapbook filled with press clippings about murders dating back some years, of which our particular case is only the most recent."

"Who would have such a thing?"

"The murderer might, if he was sufficiently creepy."

The Eisens looked at Lance. Lance kept his obsidian stare on me. There was a trace of saliva showing at the left corner of his mouth. O'Mara sat very stiffly, and didn't appear to be looking at anything. Hawk was motionless as he often was. His expression was pleasant. He didn't look interested, but he didn't look bored. He looked like he might be reviewing a highly successful sex life.

"And," I said, "I gotta tell you that Lance seems to me sufficiently creepy."

Lance spoke for the first time.

"Fuck you," he said.

"Well, that's a valid point," I said. "But let me remind you that we have your gun, and I'm betting that the slugs match up."

"Fuck you."

"Well," I said to the group, "Lance has made his position clear, but let me expand on mine a little."

Bernie was still trying to be a ballsy executive. After all, he belonged to a health club. He had a trainer.

"Nobody here is interested in your damn position."

"I know, Bernie, that you and Rowley were manipulating mark to market accounting and SPEs in a criminal manner."

I managed to do things when I said it: to sound like I knew what I was talking about, and to do it with a straight face. It made me proud to be me.

"You're fucking crazy," Bernie said. "You know that?"

"I know that you and Ellen were wife-swapping with Marlene and Trent Rowley," I said.

"You're disgusting," Ellen said.

I looked at Hawk.

"You like me, don't you?"

Hawk's expression didn't change.

"Honky bastard," he said.

"See?" I said to the group.

"You're not funny," O'Mara said.

"I am too," I said. "But we'll let that go. I know you and Lancey Pants are involved in this criminal affair with Bernie and the late Trent, because you are listed as owners of some of the SPEs. I know that you, Darrin darlin', supply black women to Bob Cooper through the good offices of your seminar scams."

"My seminars are not scams," O'Mara said.

I ignored him.

"In return for which, I suspect, but can't prove yet, he turned a blind eye to what was going on with Rowley and Eisen."

"We were doing nothing illegal," Bernie said.

"Meanwhile, in my theory, Gavin, being Cooper's keeper, so to speak, got wind, because getting wind was his job, of some problems. Something was wrong in the company's cash flow, some of the company's top executives were living sort of exotic sex lives."

"Our sex life is our private business," Ellen said.

"There is nothing illegal about it," Bernie said.

The little dab of saliva was still there at the corner of Lance's mouth. But he wasn't saying *fuck you* to me at the moment, which seemed progress. O'Mara was quiet too, but his shoulders had grown more rigid. He was probably the smartest of the group, and he might have known, while the rest of them were still denying it, that the jig was up.

"And his own beloved Yale buddy and CEO was exercising some sexual bad judgment of his own. Now, it would have been one thing if Gavin hadn't cared about Cooper. And it would have been something else if Cooper didn't want to get elected senator, and, later, president."

"I'm not going to listen to any more of this," O'Mara said, and stood up stiffly.

It was an empty gesture, and it was almost as if he knew it.

"We won't let you leave until we're finished," I said.

O'Mara looked at me for a moment and then at Hawk. Hawk smiled at him and gave a little what-can-I-say shrug. O'Mara shook his head wearily and sat back down.

"But Cooper did want to be senator, and did want to be president; and Gavin did care about him, and maybe about being close to a guy who was president. So he hired a couple of private eyes to follow some wives around and see what he could learn about the wife-swapping. Meanwhile, Marlene Rowley came to believe that Trent and Ellen had stepped out of bounds in the wife-swapping deal, and Marlene decided to secure her position in case of divorce proceedings, so she hired me to follow Trent in case he and Ellen decided to walk into the sunset together. Incidentally, clever devil, he told each of the private eyes he was the aggrieved husband so he wouldn't blow his position and bring shame to Coop and Kinergy."

They had all given up posturing. They seemed if not actually interested, at least accepting of the proposition that they had to listen to me.

"Now here's what I don't know, but seems a good guess. Things are going swimmingly for Eisen and Rowley. They know that Kinergy is going to implode pretty soon. But they are successfully keeping stock prices up, and unloading their stock in smallish batches so as not to cause a stir on Wall Street."

I paused and looked at them. Then I looked at Hawk.

"I always hoped," I said to Hawk, "that I'd have a case where one day I could use the phrase 'cause a stir on Wall Street.' "

"Not much left to live for," Hawk said.

"So," I said to the group again, "it's a kind of race to get their money out before the company went bankrupt. And they're winning the race, but Rowley gets an unfortunate case of conscience. We're destroying a great company, he says, employees will lose their pensions, he says, we can't do this, he says."

I stopped and looked at Eisen.

"Something like that?" I said.

Eisen didn't speak. He just shook his head, trying to look bemused and disgusted. He looked scared to me.

"So he says he's going public, going to tell the SEC, whatever, and, Bernie, you find that unacceptable. It'll cost you millions of dollars. It might cost O'Mara and Devaney millions of dollars, in any case, you have to do something. My guess is that you went to O'Mara, and O'Mara turned to his in-house serial killer, and Lance, of course, is about to wet himself at the prospect of indulging his hobby and pleasing his lover at the same time."

When I said "lover" Ellen Eisen's head jerked around toward O'Mara. I looked at Hawk. He raised his eyebrows and nodded. He'd seen it too.

"You didn't know that Darrin and Lance are a couple?" I said.

Ellen looked at O'Mara.

"Darrin?" she said.

"Matters of the heart know no restrictions," O'Mara said.

It was limp, but the best he could do. I think he knew it was limp. I think he knew it was all going to go south, and take him with it. And I think he had given up, and most of what he did now was reflexive motion. Ellen stared at Lance.

"Him?" she said.

O'Mara didn't bother to answer.

"And just what was going to happen to us when the time came?" Ellen said.

This time Bernie's head jerked around.

"What time came?" he said.

I looked at Hawk. He grinned. It was beginning to boil.

"When you got the money," she said.

"Money?" Bernie said.

"Ellen," O'Mara said.

"Fuck you, you goddamned fairy," Ellen said.

It was going great.

"What was going to happen when we got the money?" Bernie said.

"I was leaving you."

"With him?" Bernie said.

"Yeah, isn't that fun, I was going to troll off into the sunset with a fucking queer."

"I think I proved to you, Ellen," O'Mara said, "that I could love you as well as any man."

This time it was Lance's head that jerked around.

"You didn't say anything about fucking her," Lance said.

Better and better.

"I had to," O'Mara said. "It was just until . . ." He made a little trailing-off flourish with his hand.

"You were fucking my wife?" Bernie said. "You son of a bitch."

"Until the money?" Lance said.

His voice bubbled with something more complicated and much nastier than anger.

"What money?" Bernie said.

O'Mara pressed his head against the back of his chair and tilted his chin up and closed his eyes. Ellen sat beside Bernie on the couch. Her face was white. Her eyes looked sunken and dark.

"When you finished cleaning out Kinergy we were going to take the money and go away," she said.

Her voice was thin and flat and tinny.

"Take the money? How the fuck were you planning to take the money?"

Ellen turned the dark sunken stare to O'Mara, who still sat with his eyes closed, his face toward the ceiling.

"Darrin said he'd arrange so I'd inherit the money."

I smiled at Lance.

"And we'd get married."

I shot at Lance with my forefinger.

"That be you?" I said to him.

"You motherfucker," Lance said to O'Mara. "Have me kill her old man so you could fuck her and get the money?"

With his eyes still closed, O'Mara spoke in a voice without affect.

"It would have been only temporary," he said.

Bernie was rigid on the couch. His eyes were wide. There was a small twitch near his left cheekbone. His hands lay on his thighs, the fingers splayed stiffly.

"My God," she said. "You were going to have him kill me."

Her voice had gotten higher and she was pressing her hands against her stomach as if she were in pain.

"And you were going to have him kill me," Bernie said.

You could barely hear his voice. No one else said anything. I glanced at Hawk. He seemed peaceable, leaning against the wall, his lips slightly pursed, so that I knew he was whistling something quietly, to pass the time. The silence expanded. Time to prime the pump.

"So Gavin came to you, Bernie, and raised the issue of financial problems at Kinergy," I said. "And you told O'Mara."

I saw no reason to mention Adele if I didn't have to.

"I told Ellen," he said. "That's what Trent did too, the poor dumb bastard. He told her he was going to turn himself in."

"Ah," I said. "Of course, and, in both cases, she told O'Mara and," I shot my forefinger at Lance again, "who ya gonna call?"

"Him," Bernie said softly.

"Correct," I said. "Lancelot de le pistolet."

"I don't like you calling me funny names," Lance said.

"I don't give a rat's ass what you like," I said. "You shot Trent because O'Mara asked you to and you shot Gavin for the same reason."

The saliva at the left corner of Lance's mouth began to trickle down his chin. He started to make the wordless reptilian hissing sound again. I sat back a little in my chair and was quiet, while they all contemplated where they were. Lance looked at O'Mara. O'Mara looked at the inside of his eyelids. Bernie didn't look at anything, and Ellen looked at O'Mara.

"I think it should be Lancelot du pistolet," Hawk said.

"Like Lancelot du lac," I said.

"Oui."

"You fucking prick," Lance said to O'Mara. He managed to make the words hiss without any sibilants. "You used me to kill people for you."

With his head tipped back and his eyes closed, O'Mara said, "You like to kill people, Lance."

"You never cared about me," Ellen said to O'Mara.

O'Mara was silent for a time, and when he answered his voice was very hoarse.

"I never cared about anybody," he said.

No one seemed to have anything to say about that.

64

The silence got long. No one said anything. No one went anywhere. Lance drooled a little and O'Mara rested his eyes
some more. I knew what had happened now, essentially everything. But I wasn't sure how much of what I knew would stand
up in court. Most of the information was the result of what
some strict constructionist judge might rule to be illegal search
and seizure, and, perhaps, kidnapping. Much of what I knew
was the result of inadvertent admission, resulting from shock.
Once they got lawyered up, they wouldn't admit anything. I
thought about it a little in the silence. I looked at Hawk.

"I figure you can get two of them," Hawk said.

I nodded.

"What we have here," I said, "is a roomful of culprits, with varying levels of culpritude."

Nobody said anything. The recent process seemed to have exhausted all of them.

"Bernie, if you depart, is it possible to rescue Kinergy?"

"Maybe."

"Neither you nor Ellen has actually killed anybody," I said. "Though a jury might reasonably conclude that you conspired to do so."

"A jury?" Ellen said.

"On the other hand, O'Mara and Devaney are quite clearly murderers."

"We didn't murder anybody," Ellen said.

"We got Lance," I said to the group at large. "We have his gun. We'll be able to prove it killed Gavin and Rowley."

If it didn't get thrown out as evidence because it was improperly obtained. On the other hand we could probably demonstrate that Lance was a serial killer, and most judges will find a way to convict a serial killer. But all of that was for me to know, not them.

"And Lance will rat Darrin out." I said to Ellen and Bernie. "Which brings us back to you two lovebirds."

They both looked at me as if the ship had sunk and I had the only lifeboat.

"Or you agree to testify against Darrin and Lance, and I get the best criminal defense lawyer in the city to help you make a deal with the DA."

"What kind of deal."

"One that won't include murder."

"He's trying to divide us, Ellen."

"Fuck you," Ellen said to him, "you miserable fag."

"We can beat this," O'Mara said to Lance, "if we stay strong together."

"Fuck you," Lance said.

A consensus.

"It's our only chance," Bernie said.

"You spineless bastard," Ellen said.

"We stay together until it's over," Bernie said. "They can't make us testify against each other."

Ellen blinked. Lance hissed. O'Mara kept his eyes closed.

"Call that lawyer," Ellen said.

I got up and walked to the phone on the end table near Lance. As I passed him he lunged at me and bit my upper arm. I yelped and threw him off me and when he lunged back I hit him with a left hook that stopped him, and a right hook that put him on his back. I looked at Hawk.

"Maybe we both should get shots," I said.

Then I called Rita Fiore at home.

Susan sat up front, with me, and Pearl stayed in the backseat, mostly, while I drove to Beverly in the late afternoon, to submit my final bill and report to the managing partner of Frampton and Keyes.

"So did Rita get a deal," Susan said.

"It took some doing," I said. "There's two DAs, Middlesex in the Rowley death, and Suffolk in Gavin's demise. But she pulled it off. They testify against O'Mara and Devaney, Bernie resigns from Kinergy and explains all to the SEC. And, as far as the Suffolk and Middlesex counties are concerned, they can walk."

"Wow."

"It was an easier deal because it gives them Devaney."

"His gun did kill them both," Susan said.

"Yes."

"And the fact that you obtained a lot of this information somewhat, ah, informally, won't compromise the cases."

"The Eisen confessions are entirely voluntary, and quite complete," I said. "And Devaney's a serial killer. They'll convict him, which will convict O'Mara."

"You're surmising?" Susan said. "Or do you know something."

"Rita has been kind enough to include me in the discussions with both Suffolk and Middlesex."

"Didn't you once work for the Middlesex DA?" Susan said.

"Another DA. Another time," I said. "But yes."

"Can't hurt," Susan said.

"They fired me," I said.

"Well, of course they did."

I parked on Rantoul Street, near Cabot.

"I'll stroll the baby about," Susan said. "She needs a walk . . . and there might be a shop."

"Meet you back at the car," I said, "in half an hour."

The receptionist remembered my name when I came in.

"Mr. Spenser," she said and smiled, "to see Mr. Frampton."

I'd have been more impressed if I hadn't called earlier to make the appointment, still it was something. I sat in Frampton's waiting room for just long enough to give the receptionist's chest the attention it deserved when Frampton came out of his office to get me.

"Come in," he said, "come on in. Damnit you're a bloody genius."

I gave the receptionist and her chest a self-deprecating look, and followed him in. We shook hands.

"Well, you did the job," he said.

"I did," I said.

"Tell me," he said.

I told him. It took me maybe ten minutes.

When I was through he said, "Wow, you really unsnarled a goddamned mare's nest, didn't you," he said.

"I did," I said, "and I have a final bill for you."

He took the bill out of the envelope and looked at it and raised his eyebrows.

"And you didn't unsnarl it cheaply," Frampton said.

I didn't comment.

Frampton studied the bill for a little while, and then put it down.

"Hell," he said, "you earned every penny of it. Would you like a check right now?"

"Never a bad thing," I said.

"Done," he said.

He got out a big checkbook and used a desktop calculator and filled out the memorandum side. The he wrote out a check and signed it and ripped it out and handed it to me.

"Would you like to talk with Marlene?" he said.

"No."

"She'd love to hear all this."

"That's why I told you," I said.

"She'll be crushed," Frampton said.

"She's inherited a lot of dough," I said.

Frampton smiled.

"That will help," he said.

I stood. We shook hands again. I went out through the reception area, said goodbye to the receptionist, and closed the door behind me. I walked casually to my car. I didn't run. I have an iron will. Susan of course was not back at the car in half an hour, which was okay. I hadn't expected that she would be. At about six o'clock she and Pearl came back up Rantoul Street. Susan had some bags, which she put in the back with Pearl. Then she leaned over and kissed me on the mouth.

"Done?" she said.

"Done."

"It was pretty awful, wasn't it," she said.

"Like maggots in a trash can," I said.

"What do you suppose will become of the Eisens," she said.

"For the moment," I said, "they've got each other. That's probably enough punishment."

"Shall we go to Yanks and have a lovely dinner?"

"Two martinis and a lovely dinner," I said.

"And a doggie bag for the baby?"

"Sure."

"And then a long ride back to my home where I will make embarrassingly overt sexual advances on you."

"If it's mostly innuendo," I said, "so we don't offend Pearl, can we talk dirty on the long ride home?"

Susan kissed me again on the mouth.

"Sure," she said.